Who was this man?

He could be so gentle and yet such a bear with her.

Not that Geneva could blame him. She'd forced him into taking her up here against his will. Clearly he had his issues with his former friend. But he still must care. Why else would he go against everything, his no-women policy and his adamant refusal to take her anywhere up here otherwise?

She hadn't realized that she'd fallen behind until she looked up and saw that Calhoun had stopped on a pine-covered hillside ahead.

As she rode up to where he was standing, she saw that he was looking back down the mountainside with a pair of binoculars. She caught his expression as he lowered them.

"What's wrong?" she asked in a whisper.

"We're being followed."

RENEGADE WIFE

NEW YORK TIMES BESTSELLING AUTHOR
B.J. DANIELS

INTRIGUE

In his youth, my husband spent many hours on the back of a horse working for an outfitter in Cooke City, Montana. I fell in love with him and his stories about that part of his life. After a weekend recently in "Cooke," I also fell in love with the small tourist town nestled at 7,600 feet between Yellowstone National Park and the Beartooth Mountain Range. This book is dedicated to the unique town that inspired this book and helped make my husband the man he is now.

Harlequin®
INTRIGUE™

Recycling programs
for this product may
not exist in your area.

ISBN-13: 978-1-335-45684-7

Renegade Wife

Copyright © 2024 by Barbara Heinlein

Harlequin Enterprises ULC
22 Adelaide St. West, 41st Floor
Toronto, Ontario M5H 4E3, Canada
www.Harlequin.com

Printed in U.S.A.

B.J. Daniels is a *New York Times* and *USA TODAY* bestselling author. She wrote her first book after a career as an award-winning newspaper journalist and author of thirty-seven published short stories. She lives in Montana with her husband, Parker, and three springer spaniels. When not writing, she quilts, boats and plays tennis. Contact her at bjdaniels.com, on Facebook or on Twitter, @bjdanielsauthor.

Books by B.J. Daniels

Harlequin Intrigue

Renegade Wife

Silver Stars of Montana

Big Sky Deception

A Colt Brothers Investigation

Murder Gone Cold
Sticking to Her Guns
Set Up in the City
Her Brand of Justice
Dead Man's Hand

Cardwell Ranch: Montana Legacy

Steel Resolve
Iron Will
Ambush before Sunrise
Double Action Deputy
Trouble in Big Timber
Cold Case at Cardwell Ranch

Visit the Author Profile page at Harlequin.com.

CAST OF CHARACTERS

Geneva Carrington Beck—She had the perfect life...until she woke up one morning and turned into the renegade wife.

Calhoun St. Pierre—The Cooke City, Montana, outfitter thought he'd put his friend Lucian Beck's betrayal behind him...until Lucian's wife showed up wanting his help to find him.

Lucian Beck—He always wanted more...even when he seemed to have it all. His only mistakes were lying, cheating and stealing...with the wrong people.

Lucky—The birthday-gift puppy saved Geneva at the worst point in her life.

Mitzi—The best friend had a big heart and a greedy desire for Geneva's life.

Henry "Blade" Wallace—Blade and his cohorts Ricki "The Rat" Morrison and Juice Jensen had come to Montana chasing the double-crossing Lucian Beck.

William "Ace" Graham—The burly local biker had given up on ever getting the money Lucian Beck owed him...until he saw Geneva driving Lucian's prized vintage Ford pickup.

Chapter One

Geneva Carrington Beck pried open her eyes to find herself sprawled face down on the couch. For a moment, she had no idea where she was or how she'd gotten there. She'd awakened with one thought. Something was wrong.

As she blinked, trying to wake, her view was suddenly blocked by a lolling wet pink tongue and a cold black nose. The tongue flicked out to lick her face—and not for the first time she realized as she jerked back, her cheek sticky and wet. She stared down at the large brown eyes set between two floppy ears—one white, one black—as the puppy tried to jump up on the couch with her.

Sitting up abruptly, her head swam. The dog began to bark in little yips that would have been cute if her head wasn't splitting. She glanced from the couch toward the open-concept living-room-dining-room-chef's-grade-kitchen. Silver and white balloons bobbed as if on a breeze along with a banner hanging askew over the massive kitchen island. She strained through her throbbing headache to read the words: Happy Anniv—

Memories shoved their way through the foggy confusion. The new house full of people laughing and talking loudly over the music. The clink and rattle of ice cubes against crystal. An air of excitement all around her as she and Lucian celebrated their first wedding anniversary with the people closest to them. Her handsome husband quieting down the crowd so he could surprise her with her anniversary gift.

"*I would give you the moon and stars if I could,*" he'd said before pulling the wriggling ball of black-and-white fur from a giant box with the flair of a magician. "*But my wife's first puppy is close.*"

The room had erupted into oohs and aahs as she'd hugged the adorable dog to her. She'd been overwhelmed that Lucian had remembered the one thing that had always been missing from her perfect life.

"*You have the most amazing husband,*" her best friend Mitzi had whispered as she'd passed on the way to the bar. "*You've always been so lucky.*" Mitzi had no idea.

The memory, though, made her mouth go dry now.

Turning, she reached down and picked up the puppy, holding her close and getting another lick. As she did, she saw that she was still wearing the expensive green dress Lucian had bought her for the party. The negligee he'd also purchased had been laid out on her bed for after the party. That's when she and Lucian planned to celebrate not just their first anniversary but her thirtieth birthday.

What had happened last night that she'd ended up on the couch alone? She couldn't imagine that she'd drank so much that she'd passed out—let alone why she was having trouble remembering all but random moments from the party.

"Lucian?" With the puppy in her arms, she stood and had to take a minute for the spins to stop. Her head was a whirling maelstrom, and her mouth was Death Valley. She thought she might be sick. "Lucian?" How long had she slept? She could see sunshine streaming into the living room sliders. Beyond the glass doors the Pacific Ocean glistened blue-green as far as the idea could see.

"I love San Diego and this view," Lucian had said the day the Realtor showed them the house. *"I can see us here, Geneva, can't you?"*

She moved to the window now, trying to make sense of why it was early afternoon. Why hadn't Lucian awakened her? It had to be late given the angle of the sun.

She shifted the puppy in her arms to glance down at her wrist, expecting to see the diamond watch her father had given her for her twenty-first birthday. Her wrist was bare except for a small red scratch. She stared at the scratch, her stomach roiling as her gaze flicked to her ring finger. Her beautiful diamond engagement ring was gone, along with her diamond-studded wedding ring.

As she started to panic, she told herself that she might have taken both off last night for some reason. She looked around for her phone. The house was so large that she and Lucian often called one another via cell phone from the different levels.

Her phone wasn't by the couch. Her heart began to pound. That feeling that something was very wrong grew stronger with each step as she checked the lower floor for her phone—and her husband. He wasn't in their joint office or the media room or their gym or in the sauna or the pool outside. Neither was her phone.

At the bottom of the stairs, she looked up with growing trepidation. He could be anywhere in his huge place. Five bedrooms and five baths. She'd argued that it was too large, but Lucian said he wanted lots of room for their family to grow. As an only child, she'd wanted that more than anything.

But after what had happened with her father, she worried about spending too much. *"We deserve this,"* Lucian had said. *"I just want you to be happy."*

She didn't need a house to make her happy, she'd told him. *"You're all I need."*

There were too many places in this house to get lost, she thought as she headed for the primary bedroom with its spa bathroom, his and hers walk-in closets and a sitting space large enough to do cartwheels.

Maybe Lucian had drank too much last night and was still in bed. She recalled him making drinks at the bar downstairs, laughing with their friends. It had been their first party since buying the house. Before that, they'd lived in her apartment for a short time after they'd met because it was larger than where Lucian had been living, but she'd known how unhappy he was there.

"We need a place of our own," he'd said. *"I'm a chef. I want to entertain our friends. I need an amazing kitchen so I can cook for you."*

She thought of him last night when he'd handed her a margarita and whispered something about getting everyone to leave soon so that just the two of them could take the party upstairs. What had happened after that? The party downstairs could have gone on until the wee hours of morning—apparently without her.

As she topped the stairs, she hoped to find her husband still snuggled in their California king-size bed. She pictured the puppy and her climbing into bed with him. But she feared that she wasn't going to find him in the bed. Nor did she expect to find him on the grounds. As huge as the house and property with a view of the Pacific Ocean, she could feel his absence.

Pushing open their bedroom door, her heart fell at the sight of her negligee lying on the bed where she'd left it—the bed covers untouched. But there on her nightstand was her phone. She rushed to it. Lucian would have called. Or sent her a text. He wouldn't have just left.

She saw the time. It was even later than she'd thought, early afternoon. She scanned her phone. No calls. No text from Lucian. She tried his number. It went straight to voicemail. "Where are you? I'm worried. Please call me."

Worry and fear fought for control. Where was he? There had to be a simple explanation, one her befuddled brain couldn't grasp. Maybe he'd told her about his plans last night before she'd passed out on the couch and she forgot the details? That was so unlike her, but what other explanation was there?

She glanced at his bedside table, where he always placed his phone, watch and keys every night. All were gone, sending a fissure of worry through her even as she assured herself that he must have gone out and probably hadn't wanted to wake her.

He'd been talking about trading in his car. He'd probably been up most of the night and decided to go out first thing this morning. She wished he'd left her a note though, but it would be just like him to come back with some amazing car to surprise her. She just hoped he didn't spend too much.

She hurried down the stairs, holding tightly to her puppy as she headed for the oversized four-car garage.

"We need more cars," Lucian had said the moment

he'd seen the massive garage. *"Fortunately, I have a couple in mind."* Her father had encouraged him to wait, telling him it was a bad time to buy a car. He'd agreed, although she'd seen that her father's butting in had annoyed him.

She knew he hadn't quit thinking about trading in his older model Porsche, saying it was too much of a bachelor car. *"I'm a married man now. I need something to drive to show off my beautiful wife in."*

Geneva reached the entrance to the garage, stopped to shift the puppy in her arms and opened the door. The Porsche was gone, leaving an oil spot on the concrete floor. But so was her Range Rover. The garage was empty.

Ice ran the length of her spine, and her legs went weak with what she was seeing. She hugged the puppy tighter and closed the door, her baffled mind racing. How could both cars be gone? Maybe he'd had a friend—Mitzi's husband, Hugh—drive the Porsche and Lucian took the Range Rover. She wanted to believe it, almost did, until she looked down at her wrist where her watch had been. That angry scratch told a different story. It looked as if the watch had been ripped from her wrist.

Fear gripped her. What if they had been robbed? What if Lucian had been abducted? She looked at the puppy. "You must know where he went." The dog tilted her head as if considering the question, then let out a single bark and began to wriggle in her arms. She stepped out by the pool to the side yard and put the puppy down to do her business.

Her mind threatened to go to places she refused to consider. That bad feeling she'd awakened with sounding even louder warnings that something was more than just wrong. Once the puppy was finished, she picked her up and hurried back through the house, taking the stairs to the second floor much faster this time. She rushed into their bedroom again, only this time going to her walk-in closet and the safe hidden in the wall. Her fingers shook as she punched in the security numbers. A beep sounded and she pulled open the door.

Empty.

Her jewels, her money, everything. She stared, stunned. How? Only she and Lucian knew the code. For a moment she couldn't move. Lucian would have had to have opened it. At gunpoint? Bile rose in her throat as she closed the safe door.

Putting down the puppy, the two of them went to Lucian's closet. She didn't have to open his safe. The door was standing open. And it wasn't the only thing empty. So was his closet. All his suits, shoes and good clothes were no longer neatly filling the rich cedar-lined space.

The only thing left was one discarded old sweatshirt from college that he'd refused to part with when they'd gotten married a year ago. She picked it up, hugging it to her, breathing in his scent. Her husband was gone. There would be no ransom demand because he hadn't been kidnapped. Nor had he gone to trade in his car. He'd taken everything of value.

And left like a thief in the night.

She dropped his sweatshirt on the floor where the puppy began to chew on one ragged sleeve's wristband.

Chapter Two

Back downstairs, Geneva wandered around zombielike before the puppy began to whine. She looked to see if Lucian had thought to buy dog food. Finding none, she dug out some cold cuts from the refrigerator to pull together a make-shift meal, then took the pup out in the backyard again.

While she watched the puppy frolicking on unsteady chubby legs in the recently manicured yard, Geneva tried to think. But her thoughts circled like vultures. It seemed pretty obvious. Lucian had taken everything and left her without a word.

It made no sense. They'd been so happy, hadn't they? If he was going to leave, why would he insist on buying this house they could barely afford? Because she would be coming into her inheritance on her thirtieth birthday—the same day they would be celebrating their anniversary. The huge party had been Lucian's idea. She'd wanted something small and intimate, but he said their friends all wanted to see the house. Why not accomplish both with one big bash?

She'd gotten caught up in his excitement. After all, he'd bought her an expensive dress for the party and an even more expensive negligee. They'd been spending her inheritance even before she'd gotten it, making her worried. She hadn't even told Lucian or her best friend Mitzi about what she'd gone through with her father.

He'd had a very successful business most of her life. Her mother had died when she was two, and he'd never remarried. Instead, he'd spoiled his daughter, buying her anything her heart desired.

She never suspected that he was in trouble financially. Even when he'd been diagnosed with cancer and had only a short time to live, he'd joked about needing to die before his money ran out. It hadn't been a joke. Her father was broke when he died.

"I'm just thankful that your grandmother left you something," he'd told her on his deathbed. *"I made some bad investments and couldn't pull myself out of debt. I'm so sorry."*

She'd been able to pay the last of his medical bills and for his funeral with the money she had saved from her job at the art gallery in the historic district of San Diego where she worked. It was no wonder that Lucian's spending had worried her. While he'd never said as much, she suspected he'd had limited financial resources growing up. He'd often commented on how lucky she'd been to grow up the way she had.

What was she going to do? The realization of her situation began to settle in as her headache waned. Everywhere she looked, she saw Lucian in this house he'd loved. Standing in the doorway, asking her something, smiling at her, telling her how much he loved her, how much he loved the house, loved their life. It couldn't have all been a lie. It couldn't have.

But if true, why would he leave?

Another woman? Wasn't that usually the case?

But wouldn't he have left a note? A text? Given her some clue?

How could she ever tell anyone about this? Even Mitzi, her best friend. As desperately as she wanted someone to talk to, she couldn't bear the humiliation right now.

Still stunned, she tried to understand how this had happened. There had been no warning. No lipstick on his collar, no mysterious phone calls or unexplained late-night work excuses. They spent most of their time to-gether when Lucian wasn't at the restaurant where he'd been a chef, until he'd quit to open his own place. They'd been looking together for a building to lease for his res-taurant. He'd been so excited, and she had too. She would have noticed if there'd been any red flags, wouldn't she have? He hadn't done anything that cheating husbands did.

Because he was too good at deceit? He'd certainly fooled her, she thought as she stood in her massive bed-room, living in a house she couldn't afford and all alone.

Except for her new dog, she thought with a teary smile. The puppy was asleep on her bed. She started to put the negligee away, but in a fury, wadded it up and stuffed it into the trash. That felt so good that she looked around the room wanting to throw everything away. This house, the furnishings they'd picked out together, all of it had been to accommodate Lucian's tastes. She wanted to burn down the place and walk away—just as he had done.

Hurt and embarrassed, it felt good to be angry. She was down, but she wasn't beaten, she told herself. She still had the money from her grandmother. She would put the house on the market right away. She would be all right.

She stripped down and walked into her spa-like bathroom to take a long hot shower. But her bravado quickly abandoned her—just as her husband had. She had let the man into her heart, into her life, into her bed, and he'd deceived her. She felt weak with shame, the pain of it pushing the anger aside as the racking sobs demanded to be released. How could she have been so naive? Had he targeted her from the beginning, only pretending to love her?

She let the hot water wash away her tears. Her life had been a fairy tale, no bumps in the road. Her loving, wealthy father had seen that she never wanted for anything. After college, where she'd majored in art and art history, she'd traveled with friends who had the freedom and funds to tour Europe to see the world.

And just over a year ago, she'd met Lucian. He'd been working as a chef at a small out-of-the-way restaurant along the beach that her longtime best friend Mitzi had found. She'd introduced them and before long, she and Lucian were inseparable, living a charmed life that her friends all envied, especially Mitzi.

Now, in the blink of an eye, it was gone because it had never been real. Her fairy-tale life had been a lie, her husband was a thief, a liar, a coward and a crook. She couldn't keep pretending that she'd wake up tomorrow and it would all have been a horrible nightmare.

This was her new reality. She couldn't go on pretending Lucian was coming back any moment begging for forgiveness. By the time she came out of the shower, she was angry again. No, she was furious, she thought as she dressed, determined to do something. She would eventually have to tell her friends. She'd never had to deal with a betrayal like this. She could admit that her pampered life thus far had left her ill-equipped to handle this strange situation alone.

She needed to call someone. The police? And tell them what? Everything she and Lucian had owned had been in both of their names when they'd gotten married.

In the past, she would have called her father, but he'd passed not long after she and Lucian had married. Her father had used the last of his money to throw her a wedding he couldn't afford—his idea, not hers. She hadn't known he was insolvent, let alone sick when he walked her down the aisle. She missed him so much. He'd been her hero. Everyone had said how fortunate she was that she had Lucian after losing him. Her father had encouraged her not to marry Lucian so quickly, to take time to get to know him better.

"Are you sure about this?" he'd asked her when she'd told him that Lucian Beck had asked her to marry him. *"You barely know him."*

"I know I love him." She also knew that her father hadn't been well lately. She hadn't known how sick he really was, but she'd worried that if they waited, he might not feel up to walking her down the aisle.

"At least don't rush into a wedding," he'd said. *"Nothing wrong with a long engagement."* But she hadn't listened. Lucian had been as anxious as she was to tie the knot.

If only she could call her dad. He'd know what to do. He wouldn't say, *I told you so.* He'd take care of her the way he had from the day she was born.

Call Mitzi? She knew she shouldn't feel as ashamed and embarrassed, but she was. She was going to have to tell her best friend at some point. She felt herself start as she realized that Mitzi should have called *her* by now. Her best friend always called after parties to dish about who wore what, who said what, who drank too much, who didn't drink at all. Pulling out her phone, she checked again. No calls. No texts. It was as if Geneva was the only one left in the world, everyone else gone.

Her hand was shaking, and she was fighting tears as she called Mitzi, afraid she would burst out sobbing, but she had to find out if something had happened last night. The phone rang four times. By then, Geneva had made a half dozen excuses for why her friend wasn't picking up before the call was answered, but not by Mitzi. "Hugh?"

"Mitzi must have forgot where she left her phone," he said. "So not like her to take off without it."

"No." It wasn't like her. Geneva swallowed the lump in her throat. Mitzi was already up and gone this morning? That too wasn't like her, she thought until she realized it was afternoon. Mitzi hardly ever got out of bed until noon after a party. Not that she didn't call from bed to dish usually. "Where did she go?"

"I don't know," he said. He sounded like he was walking through the house looking for her. "I'd say she went out jogging early, except she doesn't do early, as you know, and she sure doesn't jog." He chuckled but quickly stopped as he said, "Her car is still here. That's odd." Geneva could hear the concern in his voice growing. "Maybe she went back to bed. Just a minute."

She listened to him breathing as he climbed the stairs. Hugh was thirteen years Mitzi's senior. She joked that she married for money, not realizing that Hugh wasn't going to share it. They lived in a modest house, drove modest vehicles and lived a modest life in El Cajon, to Mitzi's disappointment.

"*I should have been born a Carrington,*" her friend often joked. "*You don't need a husband. You always have Daddy's money and now you have Lucian. Talk about lucky. It's like he was tailor-made for you. Could he be any more perfect?*"

She hadn't told Mitzi that there was no Daddy's money because she felt as if she would be betraying her father's memory. She'd prefer to let everyone believe her father had been successful right to the end. The only one who knew was Lucian, and he hadn't found out until after they were married. He'd been upset that she hadn't told him, saying he didn't want them keeping anything from each other.

"Geneva?" Hugh's voice pulled her back. He sounded worried now, an urgency having crept into his voice. "Mitzi isn't here. I've looked everywhere."

She closed her eyes. The two missing cars in the garage. She knew, heart deep, she just knew. "Did she take some of her things?"

He didn't answer right away. She heard doors opening, hangers being pushed aside. "This is so odd. I don't understand. If she'd planned to take a trip, she would have mentioned it last night."

Geneva knew his confusion, his worry—worse—what Mitzi missing meant. "Lucian is gone too."

"What?" She heard him sit down heavily. "Are you sure? That can't be."

"He took everything, all his clothes, all our cash, including both cars," she said. Now at least she had a pretty good idea of who had driven the second car.

"Have you checked your bank account?" he asked.

She hadn't. They kept quite a bit of cash in the house. She hadn't thought beyond that. "Let me call you back." She disconnected and with trembling fingers called up her account. It took only a few moments.

When she called Hugh back, he said, "Mitzi took everything in the joint account and the savings account I'd set up for her. Thank God I didn't put her name on my business accounts, or I'd be bankrupt right now."

"All of our funds were in joint accounts." Was she telling him this to make him feel better? Or because she felt responsible? She was the one who'd brought Lucian into their lives. "He took every last cent."

She heard something crash and shatter on the other end of the line followed by a string of swear words. Hugh sounded like she felt, shattered more than whatever he'd broken. "I'm so sorry, Hugh. I'm so sorry."

"I need to make some calls," Hugh said and disconnected.

Geneva did the same and had to sit down. Mitzi. Her best friend. Could it have been more clichéd? The puppy had found the dangling cord of the Happy Anniversary banner and was now tugging on it. Geneva didn't have the energy to stop the dog as she found herself ping-ponging between disbelief and devastation. She'd been so happy, so looking forward to the future. Lucian said he'd wanted children, he wanted to fill this house with their laughter. Isn't that why she'd gone along with purchasing this huge house they really couldn't afford?

Geneva stood again, unable to sit still. What was she

going to do? If it wasn't for her inheritance from her grandmother, she couldn't even afford the next payment on this house. Her heart began to pound wildly in her chest. She felt faint as she fumbled out her phone again.

Earlier she'd checked their joint checking and savings accounts. She hadn't checked the trust account because she'd been hoping that the money hadn't already gone into it.

But it was, the deposit, the withdrawal. The zero balance. He hadn't let her a dime.

Lucian. He'd taken everything, including her self-esteem and left her with nothing. So where was he now? Somewhere with Mitzi, she reminded herself. Maybe on his way to buy an island.

She glanced out the front window as if she could make him materialize. She desperately wanted to see him coming up their drive, begging her forgiveness, claiming he'd made a terrible mistake.

What she saw instead made her freeze. A large dark SUV drove slowly toward the house. Unconsciously, she stepped back from the window so she couldn't be seen. The vehicle stopped and after a moment, two large older men got out. They both wore black clothing and jackets that looked bulky.

She saw one man pat his side. Checking for a phone? Or a gun? He had the look of a man who carried a weapon. Cops? She didn't think so. Geneva lost sight of them as they walked up to the front door. She heard the bell ring and held her breath. It rang again, then one of them pounded on the door hard enough to make her chest hurt and the puppy bark. She hugged the dog to her.

A few moments later, one of the men walked across

the grass to the attached four-car garage. He cupped his hands to look through the small window in the first garage door, then motioned to the other man. He didn't look any more happy to find the garage completely empty than she had.

All her instincts told her that they were looking for Lucian. She saw them both disappear on the far side of the garage as they headed for the back of the house. The doors were locked, weren't they?

She had gone out to the pool this morning with the puppy, but she always locked the door—unless she'd had too much on her mind earlier. She realized that the security system wasn't armed either. Why would Lucian bother to set it when he left the way he obviously had?

Too late now, she told herself as she moved as stealthily as possible to the guest bedroom with the best view of the pool area. The men came around the corner of the garage and headed for the back of the house. Again she held her breath as they disappeared from view under the awning over the back entrance. Were they in the house?

She reached for her phone, ready to call the police when they stepped away from the back and crossed by the pool. One of them stopped as if to comment on the pool before they both moved on, disappearing around the house.

Geneva breathed a sigh of relief when she saw them heading for their vehicle. They were leaving. One of them was on his phone. He appeared to be angry, talking fast. Leaving a message for Lucian? She lifted her phone, zoomed in on the two and took a photo, remembering something a friend had done the day before their house was broken into. It had helped the police find the men and get much of what they'd stolen back.

But she didn't think these two had come here to burglarize the house.

Her heart pounded as she watched them drive away. All she could think was *Lucian, what have you done?* Whatever trouble he was in, he'd left her to deal with it. The realization that she hadn't known her husband pierced her heart like a knife blade.

Worse, she couldn't shake the feeling that the two men hadn't given up. They'd be back. Probably once it got dark.

Chapter Three

She had to get out of this house. Rushing to her bedroom, she put the puppy down on the bed and hurried around the end of it, planning to throw a few things into a suitcase. But as she did, she stepped on something halfway buried in the thick carpet.

Reaching down, she picked up what appeared to be a key to a very large padlock.

Geneva stared at it. Had Lucian dropped it in his hurry to get away with his crimes against her before she woke up on the couch downstairs? She suspected he had drugged her. It would explain why she'd slept so late, why her head felt fuzzy and why her stomach was doing somersaults. That and waking up to find out what her husband had done to her—not to mention her best friend's part in it. Either way, she felt sick to her stomach as well as sick in heart to be deceived by people she'd loved and trusted.

As her mind started to clear a little, she studied the key, turning it in her fingers. What had he locked up that he'd kept a secret from her? And where? What if he'd left some of the money there, unable to skip the country with all that cash?

Downstairs in the office, she began to hurriedly go

through his desk. He had hardly ever used his office here at home. She found recipes he'd been given by well-meaning people who'd heard he was opening his own restaurant. Was it even true that he'd been the head chef at the restaurant where she'd met him? He certainly hadn't cooked while she was married to him, preferring to go out or order in.

He'd left behind the recipes, no doubt never planning to have to cook ever again, she thought. He could now be a man of leisure, something he must have been planning all along. As she was about to give up, she saw a faded receipt stuffed in the very back of the drawer. It took a moment to pry it out without tearing the thin paper.

Just as she'd thought. It was a receipt for a year's rental of a large storage unit. The date was right before she'd met him, only months before they fell in love and got married. He'd never mentioned having anything in storage, priding himself on never accumulating more than he could load into his Porsche. When she'd met him, he'd been living in a studio apartment, saying it was all he'd needed.

So, what had he valued enough that he'd paid an expensive storage fee all these months?

She pulled out her phone and called an Uber.

As she grabbed her purse and the puppy, Hugh called, sounding both upset and heartbroken. "I always told myself that if something better came along, Mitzi would leave me. I guess I hadn't really wanted to believe it. I wanted to believe that she'd married me for more than my money."

Geneva didn't know what to say since she was going through the same range of emotions. They'd both been duped and dumped, and it felt like a kind of death. The death of the life they'd been living as well as the murder of their illusions about the person they had loved and trusted.

"You think they're still in the city?" he asked, sounding hopeful. She could hear it in his voice that if he found Mitzi, he would beg her to come back. Geneva understood, she thought as she waited for her Uber. But she couldn't imagine taking Lucian back, knowing that she could never trust him again. She thought about her friendship with Mitzi. How could she ever forgive either of them?

"I doubt they'd stay around here," she said. "Hugh, they're gone. Somehow, we have to put it behind us."

"How do we do that?"

She had no idea. Her Uber pulled up out front. She was anxious to get to the storage shed before Lucian realized his mistake in leaving the key behind. He could be sawing off the padlock right now. She had to know what else he'd hidden from her. "I have to go, Hugh. If you hear anything, call."

"I'm just finding this hard to believe. You and Lucian seemed so happy."

Geneva really didn't want to hear this. "It was all a lie, Hugh. He was apparently only waiting for me to get my inheritance from my grandmother when I turned thirty. He planned it right down to the day."

"I'm so sorry, Geneva."

She disconnected and hurried out to the waiting Uber. On the drive to the storage facility, she tried not to get her hopes up. The way her luck was going, the storage unit would be empty. She thought about asking the Uber driver to wait but changed her mind. He let her out at the large storage unit company gate, and she headed for the office. She had no idea how long this might take. The unit could have been emptied out by now.

"Going to need to see some ID," the man behind the desk told her.

"I'm Lucian Beck's wife," she said as she pulled out her ID. "He asked me to pick up something for him." She showed him the key and the receipt as well.

The man glanced at the receipt, then asked, "What's your dog's name?"

She looked over at the puppy in one crook of her free arm. The dog seemed interested in her answer. "I don't know. I haven't decided yet."

"Cute dog." He waved her in.

She walked down the street-like lanes between the units, letting the puppy trot along, until she found number nineteen. The unit was large. What had he hidden that he needed something this size?

Her gaze went to the equally large padlock still on the door. That didn't mean that he hadn't already cleaned out everything he valued, she told herself as she checked to make sure the puppy was close by and pulled out the key.

Nervously, she tried it, afraid Lucian had already been here and replaced the lock. If the key didn't fit, she'd know that he'd realized his mistake in leaving it behind. Her real terror, though, was what she might find once she took off the lock and lifted the huge metal garage door. Her father had been right. She hadn't known Lucian. She'd jumped into marriage just as she'd jumped into buying that ridiculous house. Lucian had conned her, and she'd let him.

The key turned; the padlock fell open. She carefully

removed it and reached to lift the door and stopped. With a start, she realized that the storage unit could be full of slowly decaying dead bodies, like that one late night movie she and Lucian had watched. Lucian could have had a secret life much worse than she'd already discovered, and once she opened this door—

She took a deep breath, let it out and pulled. The door rolled up with a clatter. She blinked into the semidarkness of the storage unit, then stared in surprise at one more thing her husband had been hiding from her.

Chapter Four

Geneva squinted at the grill of a shiny black vintage pickup truck. For a moment, she thought she'd opened the wrong storage unit. Until she remembered the framed photograph Lucian had by his bed in his studio apartment when she'd first met him.

It was of teenage Lucian standing next to an old black Chevy truck. At the time, she'd paid more attention to the lanky good-looking teenager than the truck.

"It was my uncle's pickup when he lived in Montana," he'd said admiring the truck in the photo. *"It's vintage. You can't find these anymore—especially ones in such good shape. When I was a boy, I swore that one day I would own one. Just never had the money."*

She realized that she hadn't seen the photo of Lucian and the pickup since that day. Swore he'd own one someday, huh? Just never had the money?

And yet, here was the truck, where it had been for over a year, and with Montana plates on it.

She looked closer. The license plate tags were up to date and wouldn't expire for another six months. What the heck? Why had he kept this from her?

Picking up the puppy now on her heels, she moved along the driver's side to the door and opened it. She put the pup on the bench seat and climbed in, wondering if Lucian ever came out here to visit his truck. She thought she could smell his favorite aftershave.

The keys weren't in the ignition. She checked the glove box, rooting through it. No keys. But there was a paper folder with photographs and negatives in it from a time before cell phones. Pulling it out, she leafed through the photos. She'd half expected the photos to be of Lucian and an old girlfriend.

But that didn't seem to be the case. They were all photos of mountains and wild animals and Lucian and apparently friends. One photo in particular caught her eye. Lucian dressed in the college sweatshirt the puppy had clearly destroyed earlier. He stood in the middle between two other young men, all three grinning at the camera. One of the men was wearing a Montana State University sweatshirt. Lucian's old sweatshirt had been from the University of Alabama. The other man wore a Yellowstone National Park T-shirt.

She didn't recognize the other two men, but from their grins, they appeared to be good friends. Also, Lucian, who hung on to very little, had kept these photos. How was it that he'd never mentioned these men? Why keep the photos in his truck, also something he'd never mentioned? It was clear that the framed photograph by his bed at his studio apartment hadn't been taken in Alabama as she'd been led to believe—but Montana. Why had he kept all of his from her?

Mentally, she smacked her palm against her forehead. The man was a liar. Con artist. A thief. Who knew how many other secrets he'd kept from her? But one thing was clear. Like this pickup, he hadn't wanted her to know about these men or his connection to Montana, where his truck had been licensed.

She looked more closely at the photographs, all of them apparently taken in the same small mountain town with the same individuals. In one, there were several vehicles with Montana tags.

Quickly looking on her phone, she found that the first two numbers signified what county the plates had been purchased in. Lucian's pickup had Park County plates like some of the others in the photographs. She found the county online and saw that it was right on the edge of Yellowstone National Park.

Looking more closely, she could make out the name of a business behind the men in one of the snapshots. Cooke City Rock Shop? It took only seconds to find the town on her phone. She shoved the photos back into the glove box, along with some papers that had fallen out, suddenly overwhelmed by what she'd learned about her husband and unsure she could handle anything else today.

Why had he hidden the truck and the photos from her? Lucian wouldn't have kept any of this secret unless it was important to him. Earlier, she'd almost hoped that he'd dropped the storage unit key on purpose because he'd wanted her to find it, that he'd left her a clue as to where he'd gone because he wanted her to come find him.

Now she realized how foolish that was. Why would he want her to know anything about him that might help her track him down and get her money back? The thought had its appeal though. She could imagine his face when she showed up in Cooke City, Montana, with his pickup.

On impulse, she checked under the mat at her feet,

thinking it was too easy, and let out a cry of pure joy when her fingers closed over a set of keys. Lucian had never been very imaginative.

For a moment, she just sat behind the wheel of the pickup, not sure she was up for what she was thinking of doing. She glanced at the puppy happily inspecting the truck's bench seat. Admittedly, her first thought had been to take a baseball bat to Lucian's beloved truck.

It was the second thought that worried her the most. It was so unlike her to even consider such an impulsive, rash thing. Take off on a quest like this in an old pickup all by herself with a puppy to chase down her cheating, lying, stealing husband.

She put the key in the ignition. The truck started right up. She turned off the engine so she and the puppy didn't get asphyxiated in the large storage unit as she tried to think this out rationally. She could just imagine what her father would have said if he'd even thought she was thinking of going looking for Lucian.

He would have advised her to do nothing of the sort. He'd have wanted to call the police at once, to tell them her brand new Range Rover had been stolen. Foolishly, it too was in both of their names, so it might be one way to find out where he'd gone. At least temporarily. Wasn't there an app they could have set up, but hadn't yet that would allow her to find the car—and Lucian? Too late now.

She saw that her options were few. Broke, except for her credit cards, she realized that it might be only a matter of time before Lucian started using them, and then she would have even fewer options. Where was her husband right now? Somewhere he thought he wouldn't be found.

But he'd be back for his pickup. That much she figured she could count on. Right now he was probably driving her Range Rover with the money from selling his Porsche in his pocket as well as all of hers.

She could wait until he came back for the pickup, she told herself.

Or…she could go after Lucian and everything he'd taken from her. Even if she couldn't find him, she liked the idea of him finding the storage unit empty. She'd relish his panic when he found it gone and realized that she'd done something with his pickup. She could actually work up a smile at the thought.

Or she could stay in the huge house they'd shared with his ghost, wandering around lost until those scary-looking men returned tonight.

Back on her phone, she checked the mileage from San Diego, California, to Cooke City, Montana. "Is that where you've gone, Lucian?" she asked out loud, knowing it was a long shot.

The pickup, like the photos he'd held on to, had to mean something though. She had no idea what, but she really wanted to find out, because it might also be a clue as to why her husband had done what he had. She might find the answers she so desperately needed in Cooke City, Montana. She might find out who she married.

Geneva let out a nervous laugh, her mind made up as she started the truck and pulled out of the storage unit. "We're going to Montana," she announced, surprised that she was actually doing this.

The puppy gave her that cocked-head *Tell me more* look.

"It's a better plan than going back to that house to wait for those men to return, don't you think?"

The dog barked, the cutest little bark she'd ever heard, and she laughed. It felt good even though the laugh felt a little desperate and brought tears to her eyes. "I really do need to give you a name," she said as she pulled the puppy close. "Maybe something will come to me once we get to Montana."

Chapter Five

Calhoun St. Pierre leaned back in his chair perched on the narrow wooden porch in front of his cabin on the main drag of Cooke City, Montana. His feet were propped up on the railing, his Stetson pulled low, the summer sun beating down on him as dust rose from all the traffic on the narrow two-lane road just feet in front of him.

Motorbikes roared past, followed by bumper-to-bumper huge motor homes, pickup campers, vans and every size and color SUV from practically every state in the Union. It was no secret what brought the masses every summer. Cooke City just happened to be surrounded by mountains in one of the most beautiful and remote parts of the state only a hop, skip and a jump from the entrance to Yellowstone National Park.

In the middle of July, the noise alone would have run him out of the busy tiny tourist town since normally he avoided Cooke from Memorial Day to Labor Day. If he wasn't waiting on a delivery, he'd be miles from here right now, high in the mountains where he belonged.

The sound of a vehicle pulling up to park in front of the large red No Parking sign at his cabin made him fume. He told himself that it had better be the delivery he'd been waiting for. Not that he had to even lift the brim of his hat to confirm that the engine he now heard the driver cut wasn't a delivery truck.

He swore under his breath, feeling his irritation rise as he heard the driver get out and slam the vehicle door. Telling himself not to completely lose his temper on a tourist since tourists were his bread and butter, he peered from under the brim of his hat expecting to see a family pouring out of an SUV after completely ignoring him—and his No Parking sign.

What he saw instead made him think he'd seen a ghost. "What the hell?" He shoved back his hat, his boots hitting the worn wooden porch floor as he found his feet, his hands already fisted at his sides as he took in the 1952 black vintage Chevy pickup gleaming in the summer sun.

He knew that truck. He knew its owner. He just never expected Lucian would have the guts to turn up here again—especially in that truck.

Halfway off the porch, he stopped in his tracks as he saw that it wasn't Lucian Beck who'd climbed out from behind the wheel. He frowned. No way. A woman had been driving the pickup? The sight of her made him doubt himself. It was the truck, wasn't it? But Lucian never let anyone drive his truck.

He frowned, telling himself that he couldn't be mistaken. There had to be maybe a dozen of this year's vintage pickups that had been restored like this one. Maybe more. But one this color in this good of shape with that particular license plate...

"Excuse me," the woman said as he walked past her to squint at the small sticker in the corner of the windshield on the passenger side and swore. Like hell, he was mistaken.

Swinging around to face her he demanded, "Where is he?"

She stared at him, clearly taken aback, and he got his first good look at her. Late twenties to early thirties, pretty with wide blue eyes, heart-shaped face, a nice full mouth and a privileged look in her silk blouse, linen pants and strappy heels that told him Lucian Beck couldn't get a woman like this even in his dreams.

Like most of the tourists, she wasn't dressed for Montana—let alone a town 7,580 feet above sea level where the mountains shot straight up from town. The temperature today might get close to seventy but would drop to below forty once the sun went behind the mountains.

"Where is he?" he demanded, speaking more slowly as he advanced on her. "I'm going to ask you again, where is Lucian, and what are you doing with his truck?"

GENEVA HAD JUST driven over a terrifyingly narrow highway full of switchbacks and breath-stealing drop-offs that had finally led to this mountain town. That was after driving for four long days to get here. Four long days and empty long nights in cheap motels after her husband had taken all of her money, her car and her dignity.

Her chin went up. "I don't think you know who you're dealing with," she said advancing on him.

He stepped back, looking surprised, as if maybe he didn't.

"You have no idea what I've been through to get to this…" she glanced around; it really wasn't much of a town "…town to find you."

"Me?" he said.

She reached into the side pocket of her Prada bag and pulled out the photo and shoved it at him. He took it and looked down at the snapshot as if he didn't recognize it or himself. "That's you, isn't it?" she said jabbing at the man wearing the Montana State University sweatshirt.

Admittedly, the man before her didn't look a whole lot like the clean-cut, beardless coed in the picture. Fortunately, the first place she'd stopped in the quarter-mile long town, a store clerk had recognized him as Calhoun St. Pierre, a local outfitter and pointed her in this direction.

"Where did you get this?" he asked suspiciously.

"I found it in the pickup's glove box." She had to practically yell to be heard over the sound of the traffic. "Is there possibly a place we could discuss this that isn't so noisy and dusty?"

He looked from her to the photo, then at the pickup for a moment before he said with obvious reluctance, "Inside my cabin." He motioned with his head in the direction of the small log structure practically built in the road.

"I need to get my dog," she said and turned back to the pickup to retrieve the small black-and-white springer spaniel puppy. She held it close as if to protect the dog from him, which seemed to make his expression appear even more irritated.

"You live here?" she asked as he crossed the narrow worn porch and opened the door to a cabin that was smaller than a playhouse she'd had as a child. He opened the door for her to enter.

"Live here year-round."

She stepped in tentatively. It was dark as a cave inside, the log walls covered with a variety of antlered heads, snowshoes and an old metal sign that warned of bears. A shovel leaned against the wall by the door next to several pairs of skis. What windows there were she realized were covered by rugs that had seen better days.

He stepped past her to turn on a light. It didn't help much, but in the sudden glare, she took in the narrow bed, the hot plate, the potbelly woodstove and a recliner that looked like something a person might find abandoned beside the road. He must have seen her expression as she stared at the chair that had so much duct tape applied to it that she wasn't sure what the original material had been. If she'd had to guess, she would have said Naugahyde.

"I got that chair at the dump, but it's pretty comfortable. You'd be surprised what you can find there." He said it almost with pride, then waited for her to sit.

She did so reluctantly, questioning—as she had from the moment she'd awakened from her anniversary party— what was happening to her. This didn't seem like such a good idea after all. But the alternative...

"Now, what are you doing with Lucian's truck?"

"Do you have any water? My dog—"

He said something under his breath she was glad she couldn't make out as he walked over to a sink near the back door. The pipes clanked and rattled for a moment, but the cup of water he handed her looked clear. "It's the best water in the world."

She considered the cup for a moment before she took a tentative sip as he produced a shallow metal bowl. She poured a little of the water in before setting the puppy down on a floor covered with a faded Native American rug. Even worn and not necessarily clean, it looked as if the rug was worth more than this entire cabin.

"What's her name?" he asked motioning to the puppy lapping at the water.

Geneva couldn't help thinking of the morning she'd awakened to the puppy licking her face. It felt like a lifetime ago. "She doesn't have one yet. Lucian gave her to me as a birthday present."

"That right?" he asked leaning against a post at the center of the cabin. She feared it was all that was holding up the structure. "He also gave you his truck?" There was that suspicion in his tone again.

"No." She considered how much to tell him but realized she had nothing to lose by telling him the truth. "I found it in a storage unit I didn't know he had the day I woke up to find that he'd taken all my money, including my recent inheritance, and my Range Rover, and left without a word."

Calhoun St. Pierre crossed his thick arms. It was the first time she'd noticed how muscular he was or that the tattoos that ran from his wrists to his biceps were actually trees. "That sounds like Lucian," he said. "Can't imagine him leaving behind his truck though. He never let anyone drive it."

"Well, I'm driving it now," she said defensively.

"I can see that. Can't imagine, though, what you're doing here in Cooke."

"When I found the pickup, I found the photos of you and this town. I'd never heard of either. It looked as if you were good friends." He made a rude sound, but she continued. "I thought he might have come here."

He was already shaking his head. "Can't see that happening considering how many people he wronged here before he left over Memorial Day weekend over a year ago."

The timing surprised her. He'd been up here shortly before they'd met. "Unless there was something he left here he had to come back for." She saw that had caught his interest.

He cleared his voice before he asked, "Like what?"

She didn't know. The idea had just come to her. "I thought you might know."

He chuckled at that and almost smiled. "Trust me, he didn't leave anything here but the smell of burning bridges."

She realized even in the dim light this man was nice-looking. His dark hair was too long, his beard needed to be trimmed—if not shaved off—and his general attitude was definitely unpleasant. Mitzi would have called him just a little rough around the edges. But that was Mitzi, who was now with Lucian. The thought brought back an avalanche of pain that swept over her. Betrayed by her husband and her best friend, she was a walking cliché. And now she'd driven all this way to meet his so-called friend, and for what? Nothing.

"So, you haven't seen him?"

He shook his head. "Like I said, he'd be a fool to come back here. He screwed over too many people, myself included."

Geneva realized that she'd put all her hopes on finding Lucian here, straightening out what she hoped was an unfortunate mistake he'd made and putting all of this behind her. If she could fix everything, things could go back like they had been.

Just the thought made her realize how delusional she

was. It also made her angry. She'd been living what she'd thought was the perfect life, but she could no longer keep dwelling in that fairy-tale world. Even if she found Lucian and got everything back that he'd taken, she'd never trust herself, let alone Lucian. Maybe not even another man.

The puppy finished drinking and came over to paw at her until she picked up the pooch. She hugged the dog, burying her fingers in the warm fur and fighting tears. She'd been so sure she'd find her husband here.

"Look, I'm sorry," Calhoun said sounding uncomfortable and clearly just wanting her to go. At the sound of a truck's horn directly outside, he said, "That's the delivery I've been waiting for. It's a wall tent. A grizzly tore up the last one. I've got to get this one up to my clients in the mountains. So, I'm sorry, but I can't help you." At the sound of a horn, he added hurriedly, "I have to go take care of this."

Geneva nodded and rose, following him out into the bright sunshine, noise and dust of the busy town. A large delivery truck was parked in the middle of the street, making the traffic problem worse. She watched as the driver climbed out and walked to the back of his vehicle.

Calhoun followed him, glancing back once. His expression looked regretful, as if he didn't have a clue what else he could say to her as he disappeared from view.

Going to Lucian's pickup, she put the puppy in the carrier she'd bought, strapped it in with the passenger-side seat belt and climbed behind the wheel. She wouldn't be able to get out until the big rig moved. The folly of her latest situation settled over her. This had been a fool's errand. How could she have been so impulsive?

She'd driven a thousand miles over days to get here, and for what? She'd spent money she hadn't had on her credit cards and wasted time because she couldn't accept the truth. Lucian was gone, he wasn't coming back and neither was the life she'd known. She had no idea what she was going to do.

The thought of driving back down the Beartooth Highway's switchbacks was too much for her. She supposed she could go through Yellowstone National Park. She hadn't been there since she was little with friends. Eventually, she would have to go back to San Diego, sell the house and...

But with one look at the traffic heading into Yellowstone National Park, she knew she couldn't drive another mile today. She laid over the steering wheel, trying her best not to cry. She was so exhausted from the emotional roller coaster she'd been on for days. Her only thought had been to reach Cooke City, Montana, find the man in the photograph, find Lucian and get her money back. Had she really thought it was going to be that easy?

At a tap on her side window, Geneva started, sat up and quickly turned toward the sound. Calhoun St. Pierre was standing outside her window looking uncomfortable and possibly angry. She rolled down the glass, biting at her lip as she tried to hide how raw she felt. Disappointment seemed to have filled her insides, making it hard to breathe, let alone move.

"It's late enough that I think you should stay here in town tonight," he said as the large delivery truck parked behind her pulled away. "You didn't happen to book a room at least six months ago, did you?"

She could barely call up a half smile at that.

"Right," he said. "I know a few people. I think I can get you a room for the night. If you get up early, you can avoid most of the traffic in the morning."

She nodded, knowing that if she tried to thank him, she would burst out crying. Kindness, especially from this man, was almost too much to bear.

He seemed to sense how close she was to completely falling apart. "I'll be right back." He disappeared from sight, running between two large motor homes to the other side of the busy street. She caught a glimpse of him down the two-lane highway some distance away before she laid over the steering wheel again and closed her eyes.

Geneva didn't know how long she stayed like that, both she and the puppy having dozed off in the warm cab of the pickup before Calhoun returned. He handed her a key and pointed down the street to a place with small cabins. "You're in number one. It's right on the highway, so it will be noisy, but you look like you won't have any trouble sleeping tonight. There's a café back up that way." He seemed to hesitate. "You have enough money to—"

She nodded, stopping him from going any further. She was humiliated enough about her situation. The last thing she wanted was to take money from this man. Her credit cards were still working, which meant that Lucian hadn't used them, no doubt thinking he could be tracked if he did.

Had her father still been alive, she would have called him. He would have taken over, protecting her the way he always had and making sure she wanted for nothing. There were other friends she could call and pretend everything was fine, that she and Lucian and the puppy had gone on a trip, that he'd gotten mugged—could they send money?

But she had too much pride. She didn't want those friends knowing about Lucian's betrayal even though they would find out soon enough. Not to mention, she wasn't sure how she would be able to pay them back. She'd left a text message for the owner of the gallery where she worked, telling her there'd been an emergency and she'd be gone for possibly a week or two. She had vacation coming and hadn't taken it. Also, the gallery hadn't been that busy lately, so she didn't think she'd be missed.

"You're going to be all right," the outfitter said next to the open pickup window. The air smelled of pine and dust and fried food. She could hear a dog barking from the back of a truck as it roared by. Voices drifted on the summer breeze along with laughter. People came here on vacation to have fun. "It will get better," he said as if he could see that she needed some reassurance.

She could only nod as he touched the brim of his hat and headed for his cabin. He didn't look back as he closed the door behind him.

Starting the pickup, she finally managed to pull into the traffic. Driving down the street to the cabins, she tried not to think about tomorrow. Nothing was going to be all right. It wasn't going to get better. And as for luck…hers had run out.

Once at the cabin, she parked and got the puppy out of her carrier. As an afterthought, she pulled everything from the glove box and stuffed it into her purse. Something Calhoun St. Pierre had said had her wondering if the pickup even belonged to Lucian.

But the moment she and puppy were inside the cabin, she locked the door, fed the dog what was left of some chicken nuggets she had purchased earlier and put the papers from the glove box on the table.

She couldn't face more bad news. She collapsed on the bed, telling herself that things always looked better in the morning.

CALHOUN CURSED HIMSELF as he walked away from the woman. It wasn't the first girlfriend of Lucian's who'd come crying to him. Not that this one had cried, but she'd been damned close.

He told himself that he had too much to do to be worrying about her. He didn't even know her name, which was fine with him. She'd be gone by morning. He'd done all he could for her. She wasn't his responsibility. He thought about other women Lucian had hurt and swore. This wasn't the first disappearing act Lucian had pulled in the years he'd known him.

This woman seemed different from the others though. Definitely not his type. How Lucian had gotten a woman like her in the first place—even temporarily—he couldn't imagine. Well, at least she had his pickup. That made him smile as he imagined what Lucian would think of her driving it.

Standing in the middle of his cabin, he mentally kicked himself for still thinking about her, let alone his former friend. It wasn't his job to clean up after Lucian. He'd done enough of that when they were young.

He needed to get busy loading up so he could head

out for the mountains first thing in the morning. Now that his new wall tent had arrived, there was nothing keeping him in Cooke. He couldn't wait to get up to his camp. Every day spent down here, he was losing money, not to mention patience.

But his thoughts kept circling back to that moment when he'd looked up from his siesta on the porch to see that familiar black pickup. His stomach roiled at the thought that it could have been Lucian driving it. That, after all this time, he would have come face-to-face with the bastard. He fisted both hands even now at the thought.

Calhoun had told himself that he'd put Lucian out of his mind for good. The last thing he'd needed was a reminder of the hell his once good friend had brought down on him. Seemed Lucian hadn't changed. One look at the woman who'd climbed out of that pickup, and he'd known that she didn't belong here. This was a woman who'd never roughed it in her life. What had she been thinking coming here? If she'd arrived a day later, she would have missed him. Then what? He hated to think.

He made himself pack up what he could before he lay down on the bed and stared up at the ceiling. This old cabin meant the world to him because it had been the first thing he'd ever bought and owned. Also, it gave him a place to stay on his short visits to town, which weren't often. He recalled a time when even Lucian had been thankful for this roof over his head.

What had happened to that young man he'd spent so many weeks with high in the mountains? That this hadn't been enough for him made Calhoun angry. This life that he'd chosen wasn't enough because Lucian had always thought he deserved more. And look how that had turned out. Now his former best friend had become a man a lot of people weren't just looking for—but wanted to kill.

He thought about the woman again, hating that he couldn't get her off his mind. Did she even know what she was going to do if she found Lucian? He doubted it. Just as he doubted his old friend would come back here.

Unless there was something he left here he had to come back for. Wasn't that what she'd said? Something he had to get before running off to some faraway place to live out the rest of his life in luxury on her money?

He hoped like hell she was wrong about that. But as secretive as Lucian had been acting that Memorial Day weekend when he showed up out of nowhere… The way he'd gone up in the mountains, clearly wanting to go alone. He'd seemed anxious, almost scared. Calhoun swore. What had Lucian been up to?

After he'd come out of the mountains, he'd had to borrow money to get out of town. What he hadn't borrowed, he'd stolen. Was it possible the woman was right, and Lucian was back in Cooke City to collect something he'd left up in the mountains over a year ago?

If so, Lucian would be bringing trouble.

Maybe he already had, Calhoun thought, dwelling on the beautiful out-of-towner.

Chapter Six

Geneva woke the next morning to find the puppy lying on the bed next to her. She had to smile. In a matter of days, the puppy had gone from not being able to get up on the couch to jumping up on her bed. True, the bed was low to the floor, but still it was fun seeing the puppy growing. Had Lucian given her the dog knowing she would need something once he was gone?

Why did she feel the need to see some sign of goodness in the man? She pushed that thought away, just thankful that she felt much better this morning, especially after her bath. She dressed and noticed the things she'd removed from the pickup's glove box last night. What if he didn't own it? That could explain why he kept it hidden in the storage unit. Also, if the truck broke down on the way back to California, she should at least see if there was an owner's manual.

Now she sat down on the end of the bed while the puppy ate her breakfast. The owner's manual was thin, nothing like the ones in cars now. She'd found the registration, relieved it was in Lucian's name. So he hadn't stolen the pickup. That was a relief. She'd hate to think that she was driving a stolen vehicle.

As she started to see what else was in the pile, an envelope fell out. Wrinkled and smeared with dirt, the envelope looked as if it had been wadded up and tossed in the mud, then retrieved, flattened back out and thrown into the glove box.

Intrigued, she leaned down to pick it up and froze. All that was written on the outside of the envelope was one word. Lucian. But she recognized the handwriting and felt her heart drop.

Mitzi. She had written to Lucian? Mitzi had already run away with her husband. But the thought that this had been going on behind her back for some time took her breath away.

Whatever she'd written, it appeared to be several pages given the thickness inside the envelope. Why would Mitzi write him? Too afraid Geneva might stumble onto one of their texts? To keep what was going on a secret?

The foolishness of that thought made her want to throw up. Of course they were keeping their relationship secret. The two of them must have been making plans for their getaway for months. Why wouldn't they correspond in all kinds of ways? Mitzi might have been in this pickup. She might have been the one who'd wadded up the envelope, threw it on the ground, then changed her mind and…and put it in the glove box?

That sounded so ridiculous, and yet Geneva had no idea what had been going on behind her back, did she?

Throw it away. Don't open it. No good will come of seeing what Mitzi sent him. Haven't you already been hurt enough?

All good advice, she thought as she tore into the envelope and dumped out its contents. She already knew that her husband and her best friend were liars, thieves and cheats. Could she really learn anything more about them that could hurt her?

To her surprise, along with what appeared to be some photocopied sheets of paper, there was only a short note written in Mitzi's handwriting. *Thought you'd want to see this. Talk soon? Mitzi.*

Her first thought was that Mitzi had found an island for them to buy with Geneva's money, now Lucian's. Still, she unfolded the sheets of paper. There were two photocopied pages. The first was a notice of stolen jewelry. There were pinholes in it, as if the sheet had been posted somewhere. A police station?

A light bulb turned on. Or a pawn shop, she thought as she saw the name of the shop written at the bottom. It was Mitzi's favorite pawn shop, where she often went to hock jewelry her husband had given her when she ran out of money before she got what she called her "monthly allowance from the cheap bastard."

Geneva's heart began to beat faster as she saw one of the pieces of stolen jewelry items had been circled in red. She would have recognized the piece even if it hadn't been that long ago that the engagement ring had graced her finger. She quickly found the wedding band, also circled in red.

This couldn't be, but even as she thought it, she knew it was true. Mitzi had seen the notice of the stolen jewelry at the pawn shop. She'd recognized the rings Lucian had given Geneva. But instead of coming to her best friend, she'd made a copy for Lucian?

She flipped to the second photocopied sheet. It was a copy of an article about a jewelry store robbery in Montgomery, Alabama. The jewelry store didn't normally carry one-of-a-kind pieces worth six figures, it said. The shipment had been for a special buyer. Police suspected an inside job since the shipment had only come in that night. A young woman who had worked there was missing.

Geneva pulled out her phone, already knowing what she would find. None of the robbers had been caught or the jewelry recovered. She looked at the date of the robbery.

Only weeks before she'd met Lucian.

Had she really thought things couldn't get any worse? Her lying, cheating husband was a bigger thief than even she had imagined. And the woman who worked at the jewelry store was still missing? Was he also a murderer?

She felt a chill. Who had she married? And her friend Mitzi... She refolded the papers, her hands shaking with anger and fear as she stuffed everything into her purse. And Mitzi appeared to be a blackmailer? Was this note to Lucian an attempt to get money? It would certainly appear so. Knowing Mitzi, it would be something reckless she would do, not realizing how dangerous Lucian could be.

Was Mitzi even still alive? Geneva couldn't bear to think of what might have happened to her. And all of this had been going on behind her back. She hadn't had a clue, she thought as she looked down at her empty ring finger. There was still an indentation, a pale line where her beautiful engagement and wedding ring had been.

No wonder he'd taken the rings. He'd been found out by Mitzi. He couldn't chance that someone else would recognize them. But he'd also taken her watch, she reminded herself.

All the while, she had worried that Lucian had spent too much money on the rings but hadn't found a way to ask him about it without hurting his feelings. The last thing she'd wanted was for them to live beyond their means.

Geneva couldn't believe how naive she'd been. For a moment, she sat on the bed in the Cooke City cabin unsure what to do next. She'd come here to confront her husband and hopefully get back at least some of what he'd taken from her. Who was she kidding? She'd never get back what he'd stolen—not to even mention the money or valuables.

He'd taken her ability to trust. His behavior forced her into a world that terrified her. She'd driven all this way in his old truck without a thought to her safety. He'd snatched her out of her comfort zone, leaving her disillusioned and the life she'd known destroyed.

What was the point of finding him? Why not do as the outfitter had told her and leave town? Maybe Lucian hadn't come back here. But what if he had? She thought about what Calhoun St. Pierre had said about the last time he saw Lucian in Cooke City. She didn't need to double-check the dates. It would have been right after the jewelry store robbery in Alabama—not long before she'd met Lucian in San Diego.

If Lucian had come back here after the robbery, she had a pretty good idea why. Where better than here to hide the jewelry? Her husband was dangerous. She thought of Mitzi's note, convinced it was a blackmail attempt. Was it possible Mitzi had no idea what kind of man Lucian was? Not just a thief but possibly something far worse?

Or had all Mitzi been thinking about was cashing in on what she'd found out?

Geneva's phone rang, making her jump. For just an instant, she thought it might be Lucian. Her hopes soared and just as quickly plummeted back to earth when she saw that it was Hugh calling. Heart dropping, she feared the worst.

"Geneva." The way he said it, she knew something had happened.

"Is it Mitzi?" Silence. "Hugh?"

Fear gripped her before she heard him say, "Mitzi is home."

Relief flooded her. Mitzi had been her best friend for too many years. She'd been terrified that something awful had happened to her after finding the blackmail note. "Is she all right?"

Hugh made a disparaging sound. "She just showed up with some cockamamie story about being abducted by Lucian. When I insisted on calling the police, she broke down and admitted that she'd helped him leave you, but swears she was never romantically involved with him."

Such a Mitzi move, Geneva thought with a shake of her head. "I think she's telling the truth." Hugh scoffed at that. "Did he take all of her money as well?"

"So she says. How can I ever trust her again?"

"You love her. She made a mistake. I'm glad she made it home safely. Like me, I don't think she realized what kind of man Lucian is. I've been worried about her."

Hugh's laugh sounded brittle. "It would be just like you to worry about her even after what she did to you. She helped that man take everything from you and leave you."

"Yes," Geneva said. "But I'm sure he tricked her, just as he did me. She bet on the wrong horse."

"You're taking this much better than I am."

"Let me talk to Mitzi if she's there."

"She's here," Hugh said. "Hold on."

Geneva doubted her friend was going to want to talk to her. Funny how some people's loyalties shifted so easily.

"Hello?" Mitzi sounded timid, not the usually boisterous, confident, funny woman Geneva knew and loved.

"Where is Lucian?" she asked, skipping everything else.

"I don't know." Mitzi began to cry. "I swear. I didn't know—"

"When was the last time you saw him?"

"He told me to sell the Porsche and meet him back at the motel and he'd give me more money for helping him, but when I got there, he was already gone. It turned out that he didn't own the Porsche, so I couldn't—"

Geneva wasn't surprised that Lucian had double-crossed Mitzi. After all, she'd been blackmailing him, both of them just in it for the money. "You should have come to me when you found out about my engagement and wedding rings."

"I know. I know," she said her voice rising. "I just thought—"

"I know what you thought." Mitzi could never have enough money, as if that would make her feel better about herself, her life, her worth. "Did Lucian tell you where he was going?"

"He said he had to pick something up, and then we were going to buy an island," Mitzi said, sniffling. "I *believed* him. I'm such a fool."

Geneva wanted to say something snide about trusting a man who was on the run from a jewelry heist, a man who'd lied about everything and had robbed her best friend and left her heartbroken, but she bit her tongue since she'd been the fool who'd married him.

"I'm so sorry," Mitzi cried.

She knew how sorry Mitzi was and how hard it must have been for her to crawl back to Hugh—let alone come to the phone to talk to the friend she'd betrayed.

"Hugh is a good man," Geneva said. "I assume Lucian found a way to get all of the money you took when you left?" Another sniffle. "Count your blessings that Hugh took you back."

"I don't know if Hugh will ever forgive me," she said. She began to cry again. "Are you ever going to forgive me?"

"I know you, remember? You're lucky you got away from Lucian when you did. There are dangerous men after him, men who he probably ripped off just like he did me, just like he did you. Two of them came by the house before I left."

"You left?"

"It's a long story. Maybe I'll tell you about it someday. I have to go."

"I'm so sorry," Mitzi cried before Geneva could hang up.

"I know." Geneva disconnected, shaking her head. She'd always loved the craziness that came with Mitzi, the high energy, the way the woman could laugh. She told herself that they all had flaws, but she wasn't ready to forgive her. She wasn't sure she ever would be.

Only recently had Geneva become so aware of her

own flaws. But she wasn't that naive privileged woman anymore. That woman and the world she'd lived in were gone for good. She had no idea who she would be when this was over or what she would do, but there was no going back to that make-believe place.

She listened to all the traffic noise outside the cabin as she sat, trying to work up anger against her friend, but she couldn't. She knew Mitzi. She understood how desperate she'd been to live a different life. Would she do something that rash again? Probably. But with luck she would realize what a good man she was married to and make it up to Hugh.

She put Mitzi out of her mind, glad her friend was home safe, and turned her thoughts to what she was going to do now. It had been impulsive and foolish to come all this way, chasing after her no-count husband. The smart thing was what Calhoun had said: to leave Cooke City, to put Lucian behind her.

Picking up her puppy, she opened the door, considering what to do with the information she'd found about the jewelry robbery and her suspicion that Lucian had hidden the stolen property somewhere in these mountains. He'd robbed a jewelry store with three other men. The jewelry had never turned up, the robbers never caught. Mitzi had said he had to pick up something, and then they were headed off to buy an island. Pick up the jewelry? Maybe she should let the authorities know. If Lucian had come to Montana, wasn't it possible he had stashed it somewhere up here?

Or he could already be out of the country. It wouldn't be that out of character for him to lie about his plans to Mitzi.

As Geneva stepped out on the small deck in front of the cabin, she found three men, all sporting well-worn motorcycle jackets, standing next to Lucian's pickup.

"Can I help you?" she asked not liking the way they were leaning against the truck, clearly waiting for her with a threatening air about them.

"Where's Lucian?" the larger of the three demanded, trying to see past her into the cabin. There was something familiar about him, but she couldn't put her finger on it for a moment. His appearance had definitely changed from when his photo had been taken with Calhoun and Lucian.

"He isn't with me. I'm looking for him."

"That right?" he asked and took a step closer. "How'd you get his pickup?"

Geneva didn't know how to answer other than to be honest. "I stole it after he took all my money and left me with the help of another woman."

"Damn, that's cold," the man said, but didn't sound in the least bit concerned or sympathetic.

One of the other men turned to his friend and said, "You don't think he's up at the high camp, do you, Ace?"

"I'm sorry, up at the high camp?" She looked from one to the other and back to the largest one standing closest to her. "Where's that?"

Ace shook his head, all of them clamming up. "You sure you don't know where he is?"

"I don't. I'd hoped to find him here." Wasn't that why she'd driven all this way? She still wanted to have him tell her to her face why he'd done what he had to her. She needed to hear it from him. Otherwise, wouldn't she always wonder how much of it had been real—if any of it.

Also, if he'd come back here for the jewelry, she'd love to see him get what he deserved—arrested and the jewelry returned to its proper owner.

One of the bikers ran his hand along the hood of the pickup. "What you think the truck's worth, Ace?"

"Not worth what you're thinking of doing," Calhoun said as he came around the side of the cabin.

Chapter Seven

The bikers seemed a little intimidated.

"Calhoun," Ace said, "I see you got a new wall tent yesterday. You goin' up in the mountains lookin' for Lucian?"

"Nope. I'm working. I have clients coming in. Just going up to get ready for 'em."

"Lucian owes me money," Ace said.

"Lucian owes a lot of people."

"You wouldn't hold out on us, would you?"

Calhoun stepped closer to him.

"If I knew where he was right now, I'd tell you."

"And if you go back into the mountains and find him, accidentally?" the biker asked sarcastically.

"Like I said, I'm not looking for him. But if we cross paths, there won't be much of him left for you but slim pickin's. You're wasting your time if you think he has your money. I can tell you without a doubt it's long gone—just like mine is—just like hers is."

"You tellin' me you aren't working for her?" Ace asked.

Calhoun let out a laugh. "Not a chance. Have you ever known me to take a woman back into the mountains?"

"Then you don't mind if we…" He looked over at the truck.

"I wouldn't if I were you," Calhoun warned quietly as one of the bikers kicked at the pickup's tires, walking around it, still considering what the truck might be worth. "That pickup belongs to this lady now. She needs it to get out of town."

"You don't want to get on the wrong side of this," Ace warned. "Remember who your friends are. If you stumble across Lucian, you let us know."

Calhoun said nothing as the three moved on though, clearly taking their time.

"Thank you," Geneva said when the men were out of earshot. She couldn't believe how relieved she was that he'd shown up. "I was just coming to find you to thank you and buy you breakfast for everything you've done for me."

Calhoun turned to her. She was immediately taken aback by his expression. It took her a moment to realize that the anger she saw there was aimed at her.

"What did I tell you?" he demanded. "It's too dangerous for you here in this town. If I hadn't come along this morning, they would have taken your truck. You need to hit the road. *Now.*"

She was stunned. She'd been nervous during the exchange with the bikers, but apparently, it had been more dangerous than she'd thought. What was maybe more stunning was that the outfitter had been worried about her. Why else had he come to check on her this morning? Clearly, he knew more than she did about the trouble Lucian had left behind here. Just as she suspected, he knew about this high camp the bikers had mentioned where Lucian might have gone.

But did he also know about the jewelry store heist?

Though still shocked by the urgency and anger in his voice, she found his attitude along with this new information had forced her into a decision. "I came here to find Lucian," she said digging in her heels. "You have no idea what it took me to come here. You don't have to tell me that I don't belong here. But if there's even a chance he's hiding out up in the mountains at his high camp, then I'm going up there. Those men seemed to think that Lucian had a cabin up there."

"Not a cabin, a lean-to, which has probably fallen down by now."

"Whatever it is, I'll pay you to take me up there."

He shook his head. "Not happening. I've got a client coming. Like I said, I have a job, and you need to hit the road out of town before there's real trouble." He turned to walk away.

"Is Lucian's cab—lean-to in the direction you're going? I'll pay you to take me along. This is what you do for a living, right? Guide people?"

Calhoun turned back, his words coming out slow but pitched like hardballs. "Even if you could handle riding up into those mountains on horseback, sleeping on the ground, fighting mosquitoes if not bears and other varmints, I'm not taking you." He held up both hands. "Don't make me sorry I helped you."

"Fine. There must be someone in town who will take me. You can't be the only *guide* around here."

He swore again, jerked off his hat and raked a hand through his long dark hair. "I'm begging you. You need to leave here. I'm serious. Lucian isn't here, but there are

people who want to get their hands on him. If not him…
someone he might care about."

"He doesn't care about me."

"They don't know that. You're driving his pickup. Even
if Lucian is up there, your money's gone, I can promise you
that. Cut your losses. Go back to wherever you came from."

"San Diego."

"Fine San Diego. Sell that damned truck and put Lucian behind you."

Even if Lucian is up there? He was holding out on her,
she was sure of it. "I saw an outfitter sign on the way in.
Maybe he will be more interested in taking my money."

Calhoun looked as if he was gritting his teeth. "You
are making a mistake that you're going to regret."

"I already made a mistake that I regret by marrying
Lucian."

That stopped him cold. "You *married* him? You're
his…*wife*?"

She nodded, surprised by his surprise. He'd thought
she was just some girlfriend? "I should have introduced
myself. I'm Geneva Carrington Beck. I woke up the night
after our first anniversary party to find him gone with
everything. Mr. St. Pierre, I've come a long way to find
my husband—"

"It's Calhoun."

"—and to get the justice I deserve."

"Justice?" He scoffed. "I thought you wanted to try
to get your money back?"

"That too."

He lifted both hands in front of him in surrender. "I
warned you. You do what you've got to do. It's none of my
business." He turned and walked away cursing.

CALHOUN CURSED HIMSELF all the way back to his cabin. Lucian's *wife*?

He'd had to deal with Lucian's dumped girlfriends in the past, but never a wife. He tried to get his head around it. This woman had *married* Lucian Beck. Was still married to him? Calhoun hadn't noticed the telling white line on her ring finger until she'd said the words. He knew he shouldn't be so shocked. She was driving his truck. She'd said he'd given her a puppy for her birthday.

He swore as he remembered a moment this morning when he'd looked into her eyes. Gazing into all that blue was as blinding as high-altitude sunshine on the surface of a mountain lake. She wasn't just pretty. She was stunning with that long blond hair, those high cheekbones, that heart-shaped face, those bow-shaped lips, those big blue eyes. And unless he missed his guess, she'd had money before she'd crossed paths with Lucian. She had that look, like a woman who had known the better things in life, who'd never wanted for anything. She must have been easy prey for his old friend, he thought with a curse. The woman literally hadn't seen what was coming. Lucian had blindsided her, and she wasn't going down without a fight. It was a fight, though, that she couldn't win.

"Lucian, you damned fool," Calhoun said under his breath, "what were you thinking marrying her for her money, let alone walking away?" What killed him was the fact that she'd been Lucian's wife for a whole damned year. How could he walk away? It had been bad enough when Calhoun had thought that she was one of the women he'd cast aside over the years. But his *wife*?

No way was he taking Lucian's wife into the mountains under any circumstances. She needed to get out of Cooke City and as far away as she possibly could from all the trouble tailing her husband like a bad smell. She needed to put Lucian in her rearview mirror—and quickly.

Except that she wasn't giving up. He'd have thought she would have. Or called her family. Or her lawyer. Or a good friend to come with her. Instead, she'd shown up here alone with a puppy? A cute puppy at that.

He told himself that he'd done all he could do. She wasn't his responsibility. If it hadn't been for a photo taken years ago of him and Lucian and Ace, she wouldn't know about him and Lucian. And coming in that forsaken old pickup, bringing back so many memories, so many regrets, so many questions.

Calhoun couldn't believe Lucian had hung on to the pickup, he thought as he reached his cabin. He'd told himself after Lucian's last visit to Cooke that nothing meant anything to his once good friend. Lucian had hurt people who'd loved and trusted him, not giving a damn about any of them. And yet he'd hung on to the pickup?

It made no sense. Just as it made no sense that he'd also kept the photos of them taken here in Cooke City. Was it possible there was an ounce of sentiment, one scrap of genuine caring in the man?

Considering what Lucian had done to the woman he married, Calhoun didn't believe it. He'd lived for over a year being angry at the man, convincing himself that if he ever saw him again, he wouldn't be responsible for what happened. Wasn't that what scared him even now? What would he do if he found Lucian up in the mountains at his high camp?

He pushed the thought away since he wasn't going up

there, he wasn't going looking for him, he wasn't cleaning up Lucian's messes anymore. He'd been convinced Lucian would never come back here. The one thing his friend had never been was a fool. A crook, a liar, a back-stabbing bastard, but no fool. Why would he come back here of all places?

Unless there was something he left here he had to come back for.

He felt a chill. Why had his wife said that? Because she knew more than she'd told him. That thought stopped him cold. Like she'd said, she'd come a long way, counting on Lucian to be here. It had to be because of more than a few photos she'd found in the pickup.

What if she was right and Lucian was here? His former friend knew these mountains. He knew people who would lend him a couple of horses—for the right price up front. He'd also be smart enough not to come into town with so many people just waiting for him, should he return. Maybe he had come back for something he'd left here.

But if true, why had he left his prized pickup behind? Maybe he planned to go back for it once he retrieved whatever he might have left at his camp in the mountains.

Calhoun swore. But why even keep the pickup, let alone those photos? Unless…unless Lucian had left a trail of crumbs for Geneva to follow. If so, that trail had led her not just to Cooke City but to Calhoun himself. What possible motive would Lucian have for doing that?

He shook his head. Lucian was too smart, his survival instincts too sharpened, to come anywhere near Cooke—and people who wanted him dead.

No, he told himself. Lucian was thousands of miles

away by now. Why he'd left the pickup he'd held on to all these years was a mystery. Maybe he'd never been sentimental about it or the people in those photos. Surely the man hadn't expected his wife to get in it and come all the way to Montana looking for him.

No one with any sense would take her up into the mountains, Calhoun told himself as he locked up his cabin. His supplies were loaded into the back of the stock truck and trailer, ready for the trip. The horses and a couple of wranglers would be waiting. There was nothing keeping him here in town.

Don't, he warned himself as he climbed behind the wheel. *Don't look for her as you drive out of town.* "Not your rodeo, not your cowgirl."

Yet, as he drove past one of the other outfitters office, he saw her standing outside talking to Max Lander. He recognized the way Max stepped closer, leaned toward her, smiling that bear-eating-huckleberries grin of his.

"Oh, hell no," Calhoun said and hit the brakes.

Chapter Eight

Geneva heard the screech of brakes as a big truck came to a dust-roiling stop beside her. She'd been all over town, which wasn't saying much since the town was so small. She'd also been turned down by the few outfitters she'd talked to. She'd been ready to give up when she had finally found one who said he'd take her. She was just about to hand Max Lander her credit card when a large hand closed on her arm and pulled her back as if she was about to step off a cliff.

"Not a chance," Calhoun said, shaking his head.

"Stay out of this, St. Pierre," the outfitter said. Somewhere in his fifties, Max Lander was a big man, burly with a full beard as round as his belly. "The lady and I have a deal."

"Afraid not, Max. I know the kind of…deals you have with women."

The outfitter's grin broadened as he dropped his arm to finger the sidearm at his hip. "You really need to back off. The lady is capable of making up her own mind. Who's she to you anyway?"

"Damned good question." He met Geneva's gaze. She cocked her head waiting to hear his answer as well. He lowered his voice as he leaned toward her, his breath tickling her ear. "All my instincts are telling me to let go of your arm, get into my truck, drive away and not look back. That this isn't any of my business."

"Sounds like you are getting some sage advice from your instincts," she said. "You're right, this isn't any of your business."

"Can't let you go with this man." He looked as if the words were as painful for him to say as they were for her to hear.

"Excuse me?" He didn't really think he could stop her, did he?

"A moment of your time." He still had a grip on her arm, one he apparently wasn't going to give up. She let him draw her away from the outfitter, figuring this wouldn't take long.

She could see the private battle Calhoun was fighting with himself and didn't stop him. He'd been friends with Lucian. If anyone knew her husband, it was this man. If he agreed to take her up into the mountains to where Lucian used to go to hide out, then he must suspect that her husband was in the area—no matter what he said to the contrary. She remembered the change in his expression when she'd told him that maybe Lucian had left something up in the mountains that he'd come back to get.

"You can't go with Max Lander," Calhoun said finally. "Any other outfitter in town—"

"Max is the only one who said he'd take me up to Lucian's camp."

"Oh, he'll take you all right."

She gave him an indignant look. "If you're worried about me taking care of myself—"

He raised a brow, his gray gaze boring into hers. "Do I really have to mention that you've already been taken for a ride by one man?"

"Thank you so much for pointing that out."

Calhoun sighed. "Have you ever even ridden a horse? Because that's the only way to get from here to where it is you think you need to go."

"Once when I was twelve."

"Great. And, pray tell, what are you planning to do with that dog?"

She held the puppy tighter. "I'm not leaving her behind. Max said I could pay extra for her to come along."

"Oh, did he?" Pulling off his hat, Calhoun raked a hand through his hair. "Lady, you're getting on my last nerve."

"My name is Geneva. Geneva Beck."

"Like I can forget that," he mumbled as his gaze locked with hers. "So, you really did marry him?"

She might have asked why that surprised him, but then again he'd known Lucian a lot longer than she had. Apparently, they'd had a falling-out at some point. Just like the bikers and possibly everyone who'd known her husband. Some apparently wanted to find him for nefarious reasons.

Calhoun rubbed the back of his neck as he swore. "If your no-count husband is up in those mountains, he's going to pay for this, along with everything else."

"You'll have to wait in line," she snapped.

For the first time since she'd laid eyes on the man, Calhoun laughed. His smile eased the hard lines of his face and brought light to those shadowed gray eyes. She realized with a start that he really was quite attractive under all that hair and bad disposition.

She held out her credit card to him. He shook his head. "Put that away." He sighed. "If you're going with me, then you can't go dressed like that, and you can't leave Lucian's pickup parked on the main drag unless you want it used for target practice or stolen."

He was actually taking her?

With a growl, he said, "Let's go."

She turned to apologize to Max Lander, but he'd already gone back inside.

"Come on, don't make me regret this any more than I already do."

Geneva couldn't help being anxious suddenly. She'd made up her mind that she was going up into the mountains looking for her husband. The more Calhoun continued to tell her that she wasn't up to the trip, the more she wanted to prove him wrong.

But now that he'd relented, she realized that he could be right. She didn't really know how to ride a horse, she knew nothing about the wilderness, and worse, she'd be at the mercy of Calhoun St. Pierre. But she'd come this far, and she would see it through if it killed her.

After he dropped her off at the general store and told the elderly clerk what clothes he wanted for her, she and her puppy went into a small dressing room at the back, and she began trying them on. She'd never worn anything like the thick canvas pants, the skin-hugging long johns or the long slicker. It all seemed like overkill given that it was July. She told herself that he was just trying to scare her as she tried on the wool socks and the boots.

"You'll need this too," the elderly woman said, stuffing a wool felt floppy Western hat onto her head, like the one Calhoun was wearing today. Only this one was clean. "I'd tie up that hair of yours. Could be days before you wash it again. Unless you brave the creek. You ever had an ice cream headache? Trust me, dipping your head into a creek this time of year will be much worse."

Geneva thanked the woman and started to change back into the clothes she'd come in wearing, but the clerk shook her head.

"Knowing Calhoun, you'll be heading out right now. I'll bag the clothes you were wearing. You can pick them up on your way out of town." The woman threw in some feminine items and some heavy-duty bug spray, and Geneva paid her bill with her card.

By the time she was finished, Calhoun was waiting impatiently outside the store in the large truck she'd seen earlier. Only she hadn't noticed what looked to her like a horse trailer behind it. He motioned for her to get in.

"What about my suitcase and—"

"I left the suitcase in the truck. Your...cosmetic stuff I already loaded. Now get in. Hand me the dog," he said, his voice a growl.

Her new clothes were stiff. She moved awkwardly, feeling foolish as she handed over the puppy and hoisted herself up into the passenger seat. She saw the look on Calhoun's face before he shifted gears and took off as she was closing her door.

She looked around for a seat belt but didn't see one. She noticed that he was dressed much like she was— only the shine had long been removed from his clothing. They quickly left the town, taking the winding two-lane highway she'd come in on. It was impossible to relax. The truck smelled of dust and horses and something else she didn't want to think about as she pulled her puppy close.

Nor was the ride relaxing sitting on the taped-up cracked seat bumping and rocking down the narrow highway. "I thought you said we'd be riding horses?" She was looking forward to the fresh air. A saddle had to be more comfortable than this truck that seemed to wander of its own accord between the lines, the trailer behind it rattling loudly.

He glanced over at her. "Oh, we will be on horseback soon. For hours. Enjoy the truck ride. It isn't going to get better."

"Could you please quit trying to scare me?"

He chuckled. "By all means. Just understand this. Once we leave the truck and trailer and go by horseback up into the mountains, there is no turning back. No one is going to come save you if the going gets too rough. You're in it for the long haul until I take you back down to civilization." He shot her a look. "There is no whining, no complaining and, sure as hell, no crying. That understood?"

"Perfectly. Is this what you tell all the women you guide into the mountains?"

"Everyone knows I don't take women. Period. You're the first. And the last," he added under his breath. "And I tell the men the same thing."

"And the men didn't whine, complain or cry, right?"

"Not for long," he said. "The one who wouldn't stop decided to walk out. I made him pay me before he left. Never saw him again. I suspect his body is up there somewhere."

She studied Calhoun for a moment, not believing a

word of it. Turning to look out her side window, she watched the pine trees blur past and caught glimpses of a creek, the water clear, the rocks glittering in the depths. They hadn't gone far before he slowed and pulled into a wide spot on his side of the road. "Are those your trucks and horse trailers?"

"Stock trailers," he corrected and nodded.

"So, there are other people up there," she said feeling relieved and no doubt sounding that way because he shot her a look.

"We aren't going where they are. It's not in the direction of Lucian's old camp. Once we hit the trail, it will be just you and me and five horses."

"Five?"

"Two to ride and three for our supplies. There's a reason Ace called Lucian's place 'the high camp.' It's at the top of a peak two days—maybe three—from here, depending on what kind of time we make." He climbed out and she did the same, having to jump down from the running board.

She was surprised they would need that many supplies but wasn't about to question it. "What did you do with Lucian's pickup?" she asked as she followed him around to the back of the stock trailer.

"Step back," he said as he opened the rear door. Inside were saddles and bags and all types of containers.

As he started to unload, two young men came out of the woods. "Got the horses you asked for ready," one of them said.

"Saddle two of them."

The men took the saddles and disappeared back into the trees. Geneva couldn't help her surprise. She'd thought Calhoun's was a one-man operation given the state of his cabin and this truck. It had been so long ago that she'd forgotten that she'd asked about Lucian's truck when he finally got around to answering.

"I hid the truck in an old barn, but I can't promise it will be there when we get back. Word will be out about it and Lucian. Now get out of the way while I pack us up. We're burning daylight."

CALHOUN SAW THE way his two wranglers had looked at Geneva. Like him, they must think he'd lost his mind. Why was he doing this? Certainly not for a woman he didn't know—let alone Lucian's wife. Or was this about some old debt he thought he still owed his former friend? The thought didn't improve his mood.

After getting rid of the pickup, he'd used his satellite phone to call his guide to make sure the other two wranglers were almost to the camp. He'd sent them up ahead of him with the new wall tent so they could have it all set up when these two wranglers brought up the fishing clients. They would be camping and going to the high mountain lakes for the next few days. He'd promised to see them in camp before the wranglers had to leave. This was his business, his livelihood, and he was risking it all for what?

He thought about the professional thugs he'd seen in town a few days ago. They'd been asking around about Lucian, showing locals his photograph. Calhoun had managed to avoid them. But it did make him wonder if Lucian really had come back for something. Why else had the men shown up here now? Why else had Lucian's wife?

Calhoun considered the risk he was taking. Crossing the path of those bad-looking dudes up in the mountains would be more than risky—especially with Lucian's wife along. Yet here he was doing something he said he never would. He wasn't just taking a woman up in the mountains—he was taking her *dog*.

And not just any woman, he reminded himself. One completely ill-prepared for the trip or what they might get into. Worse, she was too good-looking, too vulnerable, too easy as prey once they left behind the last of civilization. That's why he couldn't have let her go with Max.

But was she really any safer with him?

She didn't seem to realize the situation she was putting herself into even now, he thought. Calhoun had an old score to settle with Lucian. No man in his right mind wouldn't be tempted to settle that score with Lucian's wife as payback. After all, Lucian had it coming.

"Two horses saddled," one of the wranglers said as he came out of the pines. "Three ready for the pack saddles. Or want us to catch up to the wrangler who is leading the clients up to camp?"

"Head on up. I've got it. Thanks for sticking around." The two wranglers would get there in time to make sure the horses at the main camp were hobbled, the clients fed, and stoves lit and wood stocked in the wall tents for the night ahead. The temperature dropped considerably in the mountains, even in July, especially near water.

Calhoun had thought about taking at least one of the wranglers with him and Geneva, but he wasn't paying a wrangler to tag along with them. Word would get out soon enough about where they'd gone and why. Better whatever happened up here stay between the two of them—and Lucian—if they found him.

"This is a fool's errand," he said under his breath. He hoped Lucian was too smart to come back here. Once they didn't find him, Calhoun's plan was to head for his own camp, where he'd get one of the wranglers to take Mrs. Beck back to Cooke City so she could return to San Diego, where she belonged.

And if they found Lucian? Or that he'd been there? Then he'd cross that creek when he came to it. But he wasn't anticipating that. He told himself this would be a quick trip and would be over soon. All he had to do was get her up there and back, and all debts were paid in full. Lucian would owe him until the day he died.

"Ready, Mrs. Beck?" he asked. She'd been sitting nearby watching him. Paying attention to how everything was tied on? Or thinking about her no-count husband? He couldn't tell.

She rose and nodded. "But could you please call me Geneva? I no longer consider myself Mrs. Beck."

Maybe she didn't, but he did, and he planned to keep reminding himself of that fact. He tossed her a backpack from the rear of the trailer before he slammed the door. "Put the mutt in there. You can't hold her and control the horse if a grouse flies up and spooks your mare and you both take off." Who was he kidding? They'd both end up in the dust if that happened.

He thought she would put up an argument. Instead, she took the backpack and slipped the puppy inside. The dog's head popped up, all floppy ears and tongue.

It was official, he'd lost his mind. "Let's get you in the saddle. We have a long ride ahead of us."

Chapter Nine

Henry "Blade" Wallace looked dispassionately at the man being severely beaten by Ricki "The Rat" Morrison and Juice Jensen. "Lucian Beck," Blade repeated, bending forward on his haunches to stare into the bloody face of the biker.

"Told ya," Ace said through swollen, split lips and at least one broken tooth. "Don't know."

Blade sighed and stood. "But you know something you want to tell me though, don't you?" When Ace didn't respond instantly, he started to tell Ricki and Juice to finish him.

"Wait!" the biker cried. He seemed to be choking on his own blood for a moment before he said, "You're right, his truck was seen in town, but he wasn't driving it."

He tilted his head and bent down again. "Don't leave me in suspense. Who was driving it?"

"His wife."

Blade lifted a brow in surprise and stood again. "Lucian got married?" That was so unlikely that he questioned whether Ace knew what he was talking about. "Who told you that?"

"Max Lander, a local outfitter. She tried to hire him.

He saw her credit card with her name on it. Geneva Beck. She's got a puppy with her."

He stared at the biker. "A puppy? Somehow you thought that I'd be interested in that?"

"Calhoun St. Pierre took her and the dog up into the mountains. He never takes women, let alone one with some puppy with her."

Blade's eyes narrowed. "When was this?"

"This morning."

Ricki and Juice looked to him for guidance. Blade cleared his throat and said, "I heard you have a beef with Lucian. That tells me that if he was in this godforsaken town, you would know where he was or where he might have gone. But you'd be too smart to keep that from me and my friends, right?" He saw the biker hesitate, only for a second though.

"Lucian had a camp up in the mountains."

"Where?" Blade asked.

Ace shook his head and quickly added, "I can tell you how to get to the area, but only Calhoun St. Pierre knows exactly where. That's probably why he's gone up there."

"With Lucian's wife and a dog?"

The biker nodded. "It's the truth, I swear."

He saw Ace looking at his prison tats, no doubt wondering who Blade and his friends were and why they were looking for Lucian. Ricki and Juice were still waiting. He personally didn't care if this big biker lived or died. But if Ace went missing, worse, if his body was discovered, it would cause him trouble. "Let him go. He's too smart to go to the authorities, let alone get his buddies to come after us. I think he knows who he's dealing with now, right, Ace?"

The biker didn't respond as Ricki and Juice helped him to his feet.

"One more question," Blade said as he pulled out his knife to check himself in the shiny blade. "An interesting tidbit before you go. Want to know how I got the nickname Blade?" Ace shook his head. "Suit yourself. Then just tell me this. How do we get up in the mountains where Calhoun St. Pierre and Lucian's wife and the dog headed?"

"WHAT DID LUCIAN do to you?" Geneva asked as Calhoun wove his fingers together and instructed her to put her boot sole in his hands so he could lift her into the saddle. "It must have been something pretty unforgiveable given your reaction to his pickup." She stepped into his hand as she reached for the saddle horn and was shot upward. She swung a leg over the saddle, hanging on to the pommel so she didn't keep going over the other side. He worked her boot into the stirrup as she did the same with her other boot. She was shaking and trying not to show it. She didn't remember being so far off the ground the last and only time she'd ridden a horse. It seemed Calhoun wasn't going to answer.

But before he stepped away, he looked up at her, squinting as if there was sun in his eyes. "He slept with my fiancée." With that, he turned and walked to his horse.

She didn't know what to say. Had someone told her that a few weeks ago, she would have argued that Lucian would never have done that to a friend. But back then, she'd thought she'd known her husband. Now, she believed Calhoun. Something told her, though, that there was even more to the story.

When it came to Lucian, she was ready to believe the worst given what he'd done to her. That was the hard part, trying to understand who she'd been married to, she thought as Calhoun hooked up the three packhorses and took the lead, trailing them behind his horse. She followed, bringing up the rear.

He only looked back once to see if she was still there. She was. His expression was grim before he turned back around, making her all the more determined to show him what she was made of. The problem was that she didn't know what that was. She'd never been tried, so she really didn't know if she could do this—especially if it was going to be as strenuous and dangerous as he wanted her to believe.

Geneva settled into the saddle, rocking along, telling herself that this wasn't going to be too bad. She checked on her puppy, who licked the side of her face, but once the horse started moving at a steady gait, the dog curled up in the backpack and slept.

She let her mind wander as the horses plodded along a trail, pines dense on each side. Rays from the sun pierced through the pine branches. She rode in and out of shadows, thinking about the night she first met Lucian back when it had all started.

She'd never seen Lucian before the night she and Mitzi went to a new restaurant her friend had found. They'd barely sat down when he'd come out of the kitchen with his white chef's coat to great Mitzi.

"Glad to see you did come back," he said smiling. *"I hope that means you like my food."*

Mitzi had laughed. *"It was your crepes. I've been dying for them ever since that night."*

He chuckled and looked to Geneva.

"This is my friend Geneva Carrington." He took her hand and gave a little bow. *"Lucian Beck, your chef tonight. A friend of Mitzi's is a friend of mine. I will make something special for you both."*

Had Lucian and Mitzi been in league from the very beginning, she wondered now? She thought about how Lucian hadn't paid any more attention to her than he did Mitzi that first night. Even a few weeks later, at a party at Mitzi's house, Lucian had been casual, polite but not overly interested in her.

"Beware of that one," Mitzi had said. *"He's too good-looking, too charming, too talented, and he knows it."*

Had she been speaking from experience? Or had she already known that Geneva was intrigued by Lucian? They'd been friends for so long, Mitzi would know that Geneva would be attracted to a man who was aloof. Too many knew the Carrington name and that it was synonymous with money. But that was before Geneva had learned of her father's financial misfortune.

Lucian was supposedly new in town. Geneva had believed that he didn't have any idea about the Carrington name. Or about who she was. Her mistake.

The next time they'd crossed paths, Lucian had stopped on the street to talk to her. It had been cool that morning, and he'd suggested they step into the nearby coffee shop. She'd felt his gaze on her, warm like sunshine. She'd been taking his measure, surprised at how nicely he was dressed. The expensive designer clothing fit his lanky body perfectly. He'd grinned as he'd suggested coffee. The smile had made her late for work at the gallery so she could have coffee with him.

That had been the beginning. Geneva, who'd been dating a man off and on, broke that relationship off. Once she began seeing Lucian, he was all she wanted. Lucian fascinated her. He'd been all over the world, had done so many exciting things, worked so many different jobs before training to be a chef. He'd climbed mountains, backpacked in exotic places around the world, swam in water she'd never seen even though she'd done some traveling herself. Now she wondered if any of his stories had been true.

But at the time, she'd been completely taken with him. He was handsome, charming, smart and funny. She'd fallen hard, but fortunately so had he. At least she'd thought so, since it wasn't long before they were practically living together—and he asked her to marry him.

She glanced down at her bare ring finger, thinking of the engagement ring with its beautiful pear-shaped diamond and the matching wedding ring also encrusted with diamonds. *"It's beautiful,"* she had cried when he'd put it on her finger.

"Only the best for you, my princess," he'd said.

She had felt like a princess—before that morning waking up on the couch alone and knowing something was very wrong. Looking back now, though, with freshly opened eyes, she wondered if calling her his princess wasn't mocking her and her position in life.

Lucian must have seen her as one of the privileged class. She suspected he had always been looking in that window, seeing what he'd wanted, feeling he could never have it. Maybe he thought marriage to her would make him feel like he belonged. Apparently, it hadn't.

She thought back on their year of marriage, starting

on her twenty-ninth birthday. Was that when she'd told him about her inheritance when she turned thirty? She couldn't remember. It wasn't something she would have kept from her husband. But had she told him when they were dating?

Geneva didn't want to believe that Lucian had targeted her—maybe even before that night at the restaurant. Had Mitzi set up their first meeting at the restaurant because she knew Geneva would like him? It would be just like Mitzi to tell Lucian that Geneva's father was "loaded." Mitzi could have even told him about her inheritance before Geneva even met him.

She felt bitterness fill her, the sour taste making her stomach roil. The two of them could have set her up. Lucian could have promised to share with Mitzi once they were married. Neither Lucian nor Mitzi had known about her father's financial misfortune.

Greed, she thought with abhorrence. Lucian had taken what money they had, along with her inheritance, but apparently even that wasn't enough. He'd had to take her watch from her father, her car, and left her with nothing, taking it all—and double-crossing Mitzi, who some might say got what she deserved. At least it hadn't cost her her life.

"You okay?" Calhoun called back to her across the three pack animals.

"Great," she said, readjusting herself in the saddle. The puppy was heavier than she would have expected, making her back ache, but she wasn't about to say anything. When they stopped, she would shift the puppy to the front for a while.

If they ever stopped.

ANOTHER TWO HOURS had gone by before Calhoun looked back, almost surprised that Geneva Beck was still there. It wasn't like he'd forgotten about her. In fact, that was all he'd had on his mind. Her and her husband. Especially Lucian.

He hadn't let his former friend clutter his thoughts—until recently when the thugs had shown up asking about him. Right on the heels of that, Lucian's black pickup pulls in front of his cabin? He'd thought he would never see the man again. He sure as the devil didn't expect Lucian's *wife* to climb out.

Reining in, he twisted in the saddle to look back at her, realizing she could probably use a break. He ground-tied his horse and walked back to help her out of the saddle. "Give me the dog," he said and waited while she pulled off the backpack. He could tell that her back was sore and chided himself for letting her bring the pup.

But she was one stubborn woman, and he didn't know anyone who would have taken care of the dog while they rode up into the mountains in search of her husband. Not without having to explain more than he wanted to share with anyone in the small, isolated community of Cooke City.

He set the backpack on the ground and reached for her hand, but as she rose and threw her leg over, he saw how unsteady she was and grabbed her by the waist, lifting her down and setting her on the ground. He could tell that she was saddle sore but was doing her best not to show it.

"Need water?" he asked already moving toward one of the packhorses and turning his back on her. He wanted to give her a minute to get her legs under her again. Normally, he would drink out of the creek, but he wasn't taking any chances with her delicate system. All he needed was for her to get giardia.

By the time he returned with water, she had the puppy out of the backpack. It was waddling around in the tall grass and wildflowers, nose to the ground. Geneva took a drink, stretched and walked around, as if trying to get the kinks out as she pretended to admire the wildflowers. He'd stopped in a small meadow. He didn't want to rush her, but they really needed to get to a spot where they could make camp and get set up before dark.

"If you need to use the facilities..." He pointed to a stand of trees before going to check the packhorses and make sure the loads hadn't shifted.

When he finally looked in her direction again, she and the puppy were coming out of the trees. She looked as if she would survive, but this was only the first day. He grumbled under his breath, mentally kicking himself for weakening. He should never have gotten involved with her. He didn't care where Lucian was. He certainly didn't want to find him. He knew how pointless it was. Closure wasn't all that it was cracked up to be. And that was the best she was going to get from Lucian.

"Ready?" he asked even though she really didn't have a choice. He laced his fingers together and lifted her up into the saddle. As she reached for the backpack, he shook his head. "I'll take the dog for a while." She looked uncertain. "I can handle it," he said, glad he hadn't said, *Trust me.* She'd be a fool to trust him with much more than her dog.

Scooping up the pack and the dog, he headed for his horse, all the time looking up the trail and worrying what might be waiting for them.

GENEVA HURT ALL OVER. The ache had started a few miles up the trail in her legs, her back, her behind. Hours on horseback, and it had all gotten much worse. She'd tried shifting in the saddle, half standing, but it didn't help all that much. Neither did leaning back. Not having the puppy strapped to her back helped though.

She saw that Calhoun hadn't put the dog in the backpack but had put it in front of him on the saddle. As the trail turned and she got a glimpse of the two of them, she saw that the puppy had fallen asleep, head resting on one of his thighs. Who was this man? He could be so gentle and yet such a bear with her.

Not that she could blame him. She'd forced him into taking her up here against his will. Clearly he had his issues with Lucian. But he still must care. Why else would he go against everything, his no women policy and his adamant refusal to take her anywhere up here otherwise?

Geneva was more than curious about his relationship with Lucian. From the photograph she'd found, she'd assumed they'd been good friends. Otherwise, why would her husband have kept the photos? But had Lucian really slept with Calhoun's fiancé? She shook her head. She'd been trying to make sense of all of this for days.

If anything, she was more curious about who her husband had been, the real Lucian Beck—if there had been one. Would they find him up here? And if they did, what was it she hoped to accomplish? She told herself that she just wanted to look him in the eye and— what? Shame him? Demand an explanation? It seemed pretty clear. He'd wanted what she had—her money, her things—just not her.

That, she knew, was what she wanted. She needed the

why. It was what kept her awake at night. Why would he give up what they had? Why not divorce her and take half? Why? Because this way, he got it all and didn't have to face her.

She hadn't realized that she'd fallen behind until she looked up and saw that Calhoun had stopped on a pine-covered hillside ahead. They'd been continually climbing for miles now. Surely they were almost to the camp. At least she hoped so. She couldn't ever remember being this physically exhausted. She never dreamed that sitting on a horse would be so painful.

But she would die before she would let Calhoun St. Pierre know.

As she rode up to where he was standing, she saw that he was looking back down the mountainside with a pair of binoculars. She caught his expression as he lowered them.

"What's wrong?" she asked in a whisper.

"We're being followed."

Chapter Ten

Calhoun swore under his breath as he considered what to do. Three men, all on horseback. Not the bikers. Ace hated horses. Could be the out-of-town professional thugs who'd been looking for Lucian earlier in the week. Could be just about anybody.

Whoever it was, they were following him and Lucian's wife. That was disconcerting. The only good news was that they were way behind. Also, they hadn't brought packhorses, which meant they weren't planning to stay in the mountains long—not without supplies.

More important, they didn't seem to know where they were going, or they would have brought supplies—and they wouldn't have been following him and Geneva.

He'd taken a couple of trails he wouldn't have normally taken because they weren't quite as steep due to the inexperience of his...client. Whoever was following them had been following their tracks, taking the same trails. He checked the length of the sun.

It stayed daylight late in this part of the country this time of year. But up here in the mountains, shadows began to fill the pines the moment the sun dropped behind the mountains. The temperature would also drop.

He'd planned on building a fire when they camped tonight, but a campfire would lead the men right to them. Unless Calhoun could get up into the rocks.

"Who do you think they are?" Geneva asked.

"Someone interested in you or your husband or both."

"I wish you wouldn't call him that."

He raised a brow. "Your husband? I'm sorry, did you get a divorce on the way up this mountain?"

"You know what I mean."

Calhoun did, but he felt he had to keep reminding himself. "I hate to do this, but we're going up the creek. It will be rougher riding in the creek bed, but it might throw them off our trail."

She nodded. It wasn't as if she had a choice. Neither did he. They still had quite a bit of distance between them and whoever was following them. But not near enough. If he could trick them…

He and Geneva were almost high enough on the mountain that his crew and camp weren't far off to the north. The trail cut off from here. It would be easy for the men following them to mistake that trail and take it, especially if they lost his and Geneva's tracks when they dropped into the creek. At least he hoped so.

He had a feeling that whoever the men were, they weren't trained mountain guides. If they stumbled onto the large camp with his crew and clients, they might even turn back since they weren't carrying supplies to go another day or two.

"Come on. Just a little farther." He could see the exhaustion on her face, but there was no helping it. With luck, they would lose the men—at least for tonight. That was enough to hope for right now.

JUST AS CALHOUN had said, they rode down a trail for a while, then dropped into the creek bed. The riding was much worse, the horses slipping on the rocks under the shallow water and making her hang on for dear life, as her grandmother would have said. The sun disappeared behind the mountain they were climbing. Darkness began to hunker in the trees.

"You said your other wall tent was destroyed by a grizzly bear?" she said when they came out of the creek and stopped for a few moments to eat some jerky and have a drink of water.

He followed her gaze to the deep shadows now settling into the dark pines. "If a grizzly finds an empty camp, they've been known to look around and end up tearing things up."

She couldn't help being nervous. It was so quiet up here. She found herself listening for any sound while she swatted at the swarm of mosquitoes that seemed to like the growing darkness.

"You might want some bug spray. You did buy some, right?"

She nodded, and he went to the last packhorse and returned with her bottle. As she applied it to any skin not covered by clothing, she asked, "Do the bears come into camp when there are people there?" she asked.

"Often enough," was all he said.

She couldn't help thinking about grizzly bears hiding in the woods, jumping out when she least expected it as they rode farther up the mountains. What was she doing up here? She was in a hell of her own making. Why had she insisted on this? As he'd said, Lucian probably wasn't even up here. It had been so easy to demand Calhoun bring her to Lucian's camp when she was standing on the main drag of Cooke City, where it was warm, where she didn't hurt all over, where she had food and a soft bed.

Just when she thought this day would never end, Calhoun rode out of the creek bed. But her hopes that they would now stop were dashed as they continued up one trail, across another and up the side of a mountain. He led them up to a rocky bluff and finally stopped. She fought tears of relief that this might be it for the day. When he swung out of his saddle and began to see to the packhorses, she almost broke down she was so exhausted, so sore, so emotionally and physically worn out.

She feared that if he said anything nice to her—let alone touched her—she wouldn't be able to hold the tears back. She thought about his big hands on her waist earlier, the strength in them at odds with the gentleness, and knew that would be her undoing. Swallowing back the pain and the relief, she swung down out of the saddle, determined that he wouldn't have to help her—only to lose her balance and end up on her butt in the grass.

He walked up to her, seeming to be deciding if she was hurt or not. The puppy lumbered up behind him and charged her, licking her in the face and making her laugh. The laugh was a little too close to a sob, she realized, and was glad when, apparently realizing she wasn't injured, he nodded and said, "I'm going to take care of the horses and set up camp. Think you can collect us some wood for a fire?"

She nodded, having never collected wood for a fire in her life.

As if he realized that, he added, "Just small twigs and

branches you find on the ground, none any larger than a foot. We can't have much of a fire."

He started to walk off as she pulled the puppy to her for a much needed hug—not for the dog but for herself. "Did we lose them?" she called after Calhoun.

"For the time being," he said, his back to her.

She buried her face in the puppy's fur for a moment. Watching him walk away, she wasn't sure she could get up. But she would get firewood, even if it killed her. She had to put the pup down to get to her feet. Her legs trembled as she stood and stretched, and her dog ran after Calhoun. "Figures," she said under her breath.

Patches of darkness had settled deep in the pines. She gathered an armful of wood and carried it up to a spot where someone had made a circle of blackened rocks for a fire near the spot where Calhoun had dropped some of the supplies.

"That should be enough wood," he said. "Here's your bedroll." He tossed it to her. It felt thin, like a rolled-up polyester comforter bound with rope. "Look for a spot not too far from here where it's flat and halfway soft to sleep."

She looked around, unmoving. Her legs ached, her back hurt, and even the slight weight of the bedroll felt too heavy. "There isn't a tent?"

"We'll be breaking camp at first light," he said as if seeing that he was going to have to explain and was irritated by it. "We won't have time to take down a tent."

Geneva nodded, but still didn't move. He expected her to sleep on the ground out in the open where anything could get her? Perfectly reasonable. "What about—"

"You'll want to put the puppy in the sleeping bag with you so something doesn't get her," he said and walked off.

Like something couldn't get them both?

"Don't worry, I won't be far away if…" It had sounded like he was going to say, *if she needed him*, but changed his mind. "If there's trouble." He led the horses into the nearby pines, disappearing from view.

Trouble? She took a deep breath and reminded herself that she had only herself to blame for being here. Calhoun had been right. She wasn't strong enough for this. Why was she putting herself through it?

She thought about her new house with all the luxuries a person could ask for, including a down comforter on the king-size bed and hot running water and walls behind a security system as she looked for a flat soft spot in the tall grass that would be her bed. She thought about her friends all snug in their comfy beds with their luxury high-thread-count sheets. If they could see her now. What she wouldn't give for a nice hot bubble bath for her sore muscles, not to mention something for the rash she felt on her behind and the backs of her thighs. Saddle sores?

Finding a spot not far away, she untied the sleeping bag and unfurled it on the grass. She fought the urge to lie down on it and close her eyes, but she wasn't sure she would be able to get up again if she did.

"Hungry?" Calhoun asked behind her.

Ravenous, she realized. She hadn't had breakfast. The jerky he'd given her the few times they'd stopped for a health break and water had done little to alleviate her hunger. She nodded enthusiastically. "Can I help?"

He eyed her, then chuckled. "You do a lot of cooking, do you?"

Her offer had been out of politeness. "No." He nodded as if that had been the answer he'd expected. "Lucian was a chef." She didn't mention that he never cooked except at work.

"You're joking." She shook her head. "He couldn't boil water. The one time he tried to cook at the cabin, he practically burned the place down and incinerated a couple of damned good elk steaks."

"Apparently he learned how."

Calhoun seemed to think about that, rubbing his beard and looking genuinely perplexed. "Guess you knew a different man than I did. You sure his name was Lucian Beck?"

She'd never considered that the man she married might have stolen another man's name. Nothing would have surprised her at this point. She started to explain why she'd never learned to cook, but stopped herself. She'd had nannies and cooks growing up. Mostly she and her father ordered in a lot in later years. Where they lived, it was too easy to order any kind of food you could imagine and have it brought right to your door.

"So, what do you do?" he asked as he squatted down and began to unpack the bag he'd dropped by the firepit.

"I work at an art gallery."

He looked up from the small stove he was unfolding to look at her. "Are you an artist?"

She was pretty sure that artists painted or sculpted or did something other than design a few things for her father's company after college. "I studied art and art history."

He gave her a look that was anything but impressed. Her father had hired her after she graduated with degrees in art and art history. She'd never wanted to be a designer.

"I've always wanted to paint," she said, trying to fill the heavy silence as she watched him take out a small pot, pour some water from a bottle into the pan and then dump in what appeared to be a freeze-dried meal.

There was something in those wolf-gray eyes that was waiting for not just more but for honesty. "So, what stopped you?"

She flinched. "Life. Lucian. I was working with him to find a building to open his restaurant." This time the look he gave her was pure disbelief. "I know, in retrospect, that must seem pretty dumb to you."

"Which part? The one where Lucian said he wanted his own restaurant? Or the one where you went along with it?"

His comment hurt, but it was so true that she couldn't think of a response.

"Don't mind me," he said with a shake of his head. "He conned me too, and I knew better, having grown up with him." He stirred the concoction in the pot and must have seen her expression. "It tastes better than it looks," he added.

"I was hoping we could talk about Lucian," she said as their dinner boiled and bubbled.

"What's there to talk about?" he asked dismissively as he pulled up two large stumps, one apparently for her. "Clearly, I didn't know the man you did, otherwise you would have never married him."

His words shocked her. "I thought you were friends." She sat down on the stump, grateful for a chance to sit down on something that wasn't moving. Her backside was definitely sore, her leg muscles feeling as if they wanted to spasm.

"*Were* being the key word here. It was a long time ago." He pulled out a piece of jerky and gave it to the puppy, who sat chewing happily next to him.

"How long were you friends?" she asked as he pulled the pot from the small stove and began to scoop food onto a tin plate.

He handed her the plate and a spoon from a small box that apparently held the entire kitchen setup. "Since we were kids."

For some reason she'd thought they'd met in college. "What was he like?"

He shrugged as he sat back on the ground, leaning against the tree stump he'd drawn up and stirred his food in the pan. He took a bite and chewed for a few moments as if thinking about it.

Hers was too hot to eat. She scooped up a spoonful and let it cool before taking a tentative bite. He was right. It didn't look very appetizing, but as hungry as she was... "This is delicious."

Calhoun laughed. "You really were hungry." He had a nice smile. She wondered what he would look like without that full beard. There was a shine in his gray eyes that she hadn't seen before as he seemed to take her in. Was there some respect there? Some admiration? She'd gone all day without whining or complaining, and other than a few times of almost crying, she'd done fairly well, in her humble opinion. Not that she expected him to congratulate her.

"Lucian was okay," he said after a moment. "We used to spend a lot of time up here in the mountains. He seemed to love it as much as I did."

"Seemed to love it?"

He smiled at that. "I guess after Lucian betrays you, you start questioning everything. But I don't have to tell you that, do I?"

"What was his family like?"

"Nice people, much nicer than mine. If you're looking for answers as to why Lucian turned out the way he did, you're barking up the wrong tree. I loved his parents. I have no idea why he turned out the way he did, and I knew him for years." Calhoun ate in silence for a moment before he finished all but a little of his meal and put the pan down for the puppy, who stuck her head in and began making slurping sounds.

"When did he change?"

His answer came quickly. "Who says he changed? Maybe he just hid what he was like from all of us. He fooled you, didn't he?"

She looked down at her plate, remembering the handsome, charming man she'd met. He hadn't come on too strong. If anything, he'd seemed unwilling to get involved. Had that been part of the appeal? He'd seem to want nothing from her.

"Why did he go to college in Alabama instead of Montana?" she asked as she watched Calhoun fill the small pot with water, put it back on the stove and collect her plate and spoon to wash the dishes.

"He got a scholarship to play basketball. He was good. Then, like a lot of players, he got hurt and ended up quitting the team and later dropping out just before graduation."

She thought about him not finishing college. "What was he majoring in?"

"Journalism. He always talked about being a foreign

correspondent. Was into politics. He wanted to travel. He resented kids whose parents paid for them to go to Europe after high school or let them take off on trips around the US." He began to wash the dishes, putting them into a canvas bag. "He always wanted to go somewhere, so he went to Alabama to school. Far as I know, he didn't get much farther."

She thought about the stories he told of his experiences around the world. Lies? "But he came back to Cooke City?"

The outfitter looked at her as if he wished he hadn't said anything if she was going to keep peppering him with questions. "We'd always spent summers up here. He hadn't been here for a couple of years. Then he showed up Memorial Day weekend just over a year ago."

She couldn't understand why Lucian had given up on his dream. "Did he tell you why he quit college so close to graduation?"

"I never asked." He rose and put away everything from their dinner. "We ride before daybreak. You should get some sleep."

"What if a bear comes into camp?"

He chuckled. "Oh, you'll know, don't worry about that." He took the portable kitchen to one of the packs and came back with a bedroll much like the one he'd given her.

She watched him spread it out before lying down, his back to her. "I can't believe you're just going to sleep. What about the men you said were following us?"

"We lost them for now, and it's dark."

"But once they realize—"

He rolled back over to face her. "They won't attack

in the dark, not up here on this cliff, not until daylight. So how about you let me get some sleep until then."

She nodded although that made no sense to her at all. He rolled back over, and within seconds, she heard him snoring.

WHEN HAD LUCIAN CHANGED? The question kept Calhoun awake as he pretended to snore to shut up the man's wife. After Lucian's junior year in college in Alabama, Calhoun had gotten the feeling that he'd fallen in with some rough friends.

The change had been subtle at first. Lucian had always loved Cooke City and the great outdoors, so when he was back the first couple of years for the summer, he seemed almost the same. The area challenged a man with its steep peaks, rough terrain, uncertain weather and wild animals. There was so much up here that could kill you. That's why you had to put any personal problems aside when in the mountains. You had to always be alert for danger.

Calhoun couldn't help seeing an even greater change the last time he'd seen his old friend. Lucian had been nervous, anxious to get up into the mountains. He'd insisted on taking off on his own, something Calhoun had advised him against, and yet Lucian had gone anyway, as if he couldn't wait. Or as if something or someone was after him.

"*Want to tell me what kind of trouble you're in?*" Calhoun remembered asking him.

Lucian had laughed, waving it off, but Calhoun hadn't been fooled. He'd told himself that he knew the man too well. Lucian was in trouble.

"If there is anything I can do to help..." he'd offered.

"Best to stay as far away from me as you can," his friend had said. *"Right now, I'm Typhoid Mary."*

"I doubt whatever you have is catching."

"You might be surprised."

"How contagious are we talking?" he'd asked, afraid of what Lucian had brought to Cooke.

"Don't worry, I'll be gone before you start seeing any symptoms."

Lucian had gone up into the mountains. Calhoun had clients he had to take to a series of high mountain lakes for a five-day fishing and camping trip. By the time he returned to town, his friend was gone, leaving a path of destruction in his wake. In a matter of days, Lucian had burned every bridge, cheating everyone he knew and some he'd just met.

It wasn't until a few weeks later that Calhoun learned what else Lucian had done—this time to his supposedly good friend. Calhoun still couldn't understand why, but in the long run, his old friend had done him a favor by sleeping with his fiancée.

He'd known the moment he walked in the door at her apartment in Billings and saw Dana's face. His expression must have given him away as well, because she had burst into tears, assuming Lucian had told him.

"It just happened," she'd confessed. "Lucian stopped by on his way out of state. He seemed so sad and scared. I felt so bad for him, and I guess I just wanted to..."

He wasn't sure what Dana had wanted to do. He'd never asked. He'd walked out and hadn't looked back. Instead, he'd gone looking for Lucian but hadn't found him, which, looking back, was also a blessing. He feared what he might have done.

That Lucian could betray him like that felt more than personal. His friend had taken a chainsaw to the ties that had bound them for years. It was as if he was sending him a message. Calhoun had gotten it loud and clear. Their friendship was over, smoldering in the ruins that Lucian had left behind.

He'd been convinced that Lucian's treachery against him meant he would never show his face around Cooke City ever again. Calhoun had never dreamed that the painful reminder of Lucian's betrayal would come in the shapely form of Geneva Carrington Beck driving up in her husband's prized pickup.

Calhoun closed his eyes, needing sleep so he didn't spend the dark hours mentally kicking himself for what he'd already done by bringing Geneva up here—and for what he might do before this excursion was over.

Chapter Eleven

Moving her sleeping bag a little closer to his, Geneva spread it out and laid down as he had done. The ground was hard under her, some of the wildflower stems poking her through the thin stuffing. She realized that he'd had her collect firewood, but he'd never built a fire. He'd just been trying to keep her out of his hair.

Grumbling under her breath, she rolled over on her back, telling herself that she would never be able to sleep. She'd never in her life slept outdoors, she thought, listening for bears. All she could hear were mosquitoes buzzing around her. Swarming really, making it hard not to swallow some of them.

Her eyes focused on the star-filled sky through the pine branches and she was struck with awe. She'd never in her life seen a sky like that. The stars looked so close she felt as if she could touch them.

Breathing in the cold night air, she snuggled deeper in the bag, the puppy next to her. The quiet felt intense. She could hear the faint breeze whispering in the tops of the pine boughs and Calhoun softly snoring. One of the horses moved, shuddered and then fell silent again.

Geneva hated to close her eyes, the stars were so magnificent, but she must have because it seemed only moments later that she awoke to Calhoun packing up the horses. A sliver of orange outlined the black of mountains to the east as the sun slowly scaled the backside, harkening daylight. She hurriedly wiggled out of her sleeping bag and rose. Her body ached as if she'd been beaten with a bat. She saw that her puppy was already up. The dog came waddling over to her. Geneva bent down to pet her and got a reassuring lick.

"I fed her," Calhoun said without looking at her.

"Thank you." She stretched, trying to work out the kinks. It was the first time she'd ever slept in all her clothes—except for the night Lucian left her, she corrected.

Calhoun finally turned to look at her. He actually seemed to see her. "Good morning."

Unconsciously, she raked a hand through her hair and quickly tied it up. His greeting surprised her. It was the most pleasant he'd been, especially in the morning.

She needed to pee, but she was also desperate to wash her face and brush her teeth. "May I have my makeup bag, please?"

He made a disgruntled sound. "Make it quick," he added gruffly, and he went to the closest packhorse to pull out her toiletries.

Taking it, she headed for the creek. As she cut through the pines, she looked back, wondering how far she'd have to go to get the privacy she needed. She had to follow the creek a few yards downstream before she could no longer see Calhoun or the horses or the camp.

Stepping away from the creek, she did her business, then had just began to wash her face in the freezing cold water when she heard a rumble in the distance. She looked in the direction it had come from. Thunder?

A thin light had turned the darkness to the east to twilight. But something darker rimmed the peaks. A thunderstorm?

"COME ON, we have to get moving," Calhoun said as she hurriedly returned. He took her makeup bag and stuffed it into one of the panniers on the packhorse. "I'll take the puppy. There's a storm headed this way. We need to try to get to shelter before it hits. We probably won't, so prepare for some cold, wet water."

He tossed her the long yellow coat the clerk had called a slicker. She shrugged into it, feeling his sense of urgency. Was he saying they were going back to town? She had to admit, the idea had its appeal. She still felt the effects of the long horseback ride and sleeping on the ground last night. Her desire to face her duplicitous husband was fading fast at the thought of another long day in the saddle, let alone being caught in a thunderstorm.

"Use that log over there to mount your horse. I might not always be around."

Before she could ask him what that meant, he was scooping up the puppy and heading for his horse.

Geneva led her already saddled horse over to the fallen log he'd indicated and used it to swing up into the saddle. She couldn't help grinning because she'd done it. Still, his words worried her. In case he wasn't around? She really didn't like the sound of that.

She quickly realized that they weren't heading back to Cooke City. Instead, they climbed higher, the trail more rugged and rocky, as the dark, ominous storm clouds gathered in the mountains ahead of them. To her, it appeared they were headed right into the tempest—as if that wasn't what they'd been doing coming up here to begin with. Why had this seemed like a good idea?

Geneva didn't know how long they'd been in the saddle before she felt a large raindrop hit her in the face, then another. She pulled the brim of her hat forward as the sky opened up, dumping icy rain and darkness with a fury of sound like none she'd ever heard. The mountain seemed to shudder under the inundation of pounding rain and thunderous booms. Lightning splintered the darkness in blinding flashes.

Geneva bent over her horse, hanging on in terror that the storm would spook the mare and it would take off, unseating her. She couldn't bear the thought of being bucked off since she feared it would break every bone in her body when she hit the ground.

When Calhoun finally stopped, she felt such a flood of relief that she had to choke back tears. He helped her down from her horse, taking the reins and pointing toward the large boulder above them. She had to lean into him to hear what he was saying. All she caught was the word "cave" before she took the soaked and trembling puppy from him and worked her way up the slippery slope to find shelter back under the rock.

The space provided little head room but was spacious enough that she could have laid down. Something she definitely thought about. She was cold and damp and tired. She hugged the wet puppy, slipping her under her slicker as she tried to warm up the little dog. There was a firepit someone had made with a circle of small rocks and some dry wood, but she had no way of starting a fire. Something else she'd never done. The list just kept getting longer.

Calhoun was gone for so long that she began to fear that he'd left her here to die. She'd never been so happy to see anyone as he ducked into the cave, dragging a large canvas bag behind him. He looked at her huddled over the puppy shivering and quickly began to build a fire. "You're going to have to get out of your wet clothing." It took him only a few moments to get a fire going. The smoke rose to escape through a crack in the rock above them. "Give me the dog."

Reluctantly, she handed over the puppy but hesitated to take off her clothing. The slicker had kept most of the water off of her, but still the pouring rain had soaked her canvas pants and her base-layer top. While the space was large enough for both of them, there was no privacy.

Calhoun looked at her and groaned. "If you think I'm going out in the rain while you change…" He didn't finish as he pulled out what she recognized as long johns and a long-sleeved top. He tossed them to her and shook his head, pulled the puppy close to him and turned his back to her.

Geneva quickly changed out of her wet clothing and put on the way too large long underwear. "Done." She crossed her arms over her chest as she noticed her hard nipples pressed against the fabric. "Thanks."

He shook his head at her as he pulled a woolen vest out of the bag and handed that to her as well. Before she could put it on, he stripped off his wet T-shirt.

There was no place for her to turn away unless she wanted to stare at the stone wall of rock directly behind her. She reached for the puppy, brushing Calhoun's arm as he dropped the wet shirt on the bag he'd brought in. He stopped to peer at her as she quickly averted her eyes from his bare chest.

"What's so funny?" she demanded as he began to laugh.

"You. I'm just trying to imagine you and Lucian together. He must have smoothed off a lot of his rough edges to get you to marry him. Clearly, stripping down in the wilds isn't something the two of you did."

"Excuse me?" There was no reason to argue. She and Lucian hadn't spent any time in the wilds—let alone gotten naked in a cave in the woods. She could hear the thunderstorm moving off, but the rain now fell in a steady curtain just beyond Calhoun. "I'm not a prude."

He lifted an eyebrow at that.

"Because I didn't want to get naked in front of you?"

"Because you'd rather die of hypothermia than change your clothing with me here. Worse, you'd rather I freeze to death than make you uncomfortable by taking off my wet clothes," he said, kicking off his boots. "But princess, that isn't going to happen. You might want to avert your eyes." He stripped off his jeans.

Of course, he went commando. She dropped her gaze to the puppy even as she felt his gaze warm her cheeks. He was enjoying her discomfort. She kept her eyes averted, feeling foolish because some of the heat in her cheeks had nothing to do with embarrassment.

From what she'd inadvertently seen, Calhoun St. Pierre had an amazing body, muscular and quite impressive. She wished she was the kind of woman who could have openly appreciated it and this complicated man. Maybe he was right. Maybe she was a prude. She'd only had a few boyfriends before Lucian, only one of them serious enough that she'd slept with him.

"*I can't believe how inexperienced you are,*" Mitzi had laughed the night the two of them had drank too much and she'd confessed she'd been with only one other man besides Lucian. "*If you tell me that you were saving yourself for marriage—*"

"*I wasn't. I just never met anyone I wanted to get that intimate with,*" Geneva had said.

"*It's just sex,*" Mitzi had said with a laugh.

"*Not for me.*"

"*OMG, you really are a prude.*"

Apparently so, she thought now.

"I'm sorry," the outfitter said.

She looked up as Calhoun sat back down, now dressed in a pair of canvas pants and a long-sleeved T-shirt. He held his hands over the fire before glancing out of the cave. The rain was letting up.

When he turned back, his gaze met hers. "I shouldn't have made fun of you."

"It's okay, you're right. I am a prude."

He shrugged, his gaze still holding hers. "I never thought I'd be jealous of Lucian." He chuckled.

It took her a moment to realize what he'd said. Was that a compliment? She stared into his wolf-like gray eyes, her heart kicking up a beat. The heat from the fire warmed her cheeks. So did the way he was looking at her.

Before she could react, he reached over and brushed a lock of her wet hair back from her cheek. Those gray eyes seemed to pin her to the spot. She couldn't have moved if she wanted to. Nor could she breathe as his thumb found its way to her lips, the callused pad rough, the friction sending heat lightning arcing through her. A new heat raced along her veins to her center.

As he drew his hand back, she swallowed the lump that had risen in her throat. Her nipples were hard, only this time not from the cold. She started to cross her arms again, afraid he'd see her reaction to his touch, to that way he had of looking at her when it wasn't anger he was feeling, and remembered the vest he'd handed her. She quickly put it on.

He cleared his throat, seemingly as uncomfortable as she felt. Uncomfortable and yet drawn to this man in a way that sent goose bumps racing across her skin. "The rain's stopped. We need to get moving," he said, but didn't move.

She looked into his eyes, shocked to realize how badly she wanted him to touch her again. She didn't question her motives, but it had nothing to do with getting back at her no-count husband.

Calhoun broke eye contact with a curse and began putting out the fire. "The sun can dry our clothing on the way. In the meantime…" He pulled out the second pair of canvas pants he'd made her buy and handed them to her. As he did, his gaze went to her chest. "You can keep the vest on until it warms up."

With that, he turned and ducked out of the cave. Her puppy wiggled out of her arms and went after him. Apparently, she wasn't the only one Calhoun St. Pierre was growing on.

BLADE SHOOK THE rainwater from his hat. They'd lost valuable time being forced to take shelter under a stand of pines to wait out the storm. Not to mention that cold night they'd spent huddled by the fire. He told himself that Lucian wouldn't have been going anywhere in that downpour either. Or in the dark last night. If the man was still up here in these mountains, they would find him.

He could hear Ricki and Juice complaining. They should have brought more clothing, something to eat other than jerky. What did they know about Montana weather in the summer high in the mountains? They were Alabama born and raised and damned proud of it. Blade had thought they would have reached the camp by now, found Lucian, finished their business and be headed back to town a long time ago.

"Juice needs to get warmed up," Ricki said as he rode his horse up to him. "He wants to build a fire and dry out his clothes."

"We're all drenched. There's no time. The sun will have to warm us up." He turned in his saddle to look back at Juice, who was visibly shivering next to his horse. "The sooner we get to the camp, the sooner we can get back to town and have a big Montana steak. Saddle up."

He saw Juice's expression and thought for a minute that the man would argue. Blade figured if he did, he'd shoot him where he stood. He'd had enough of both his and Ricki's complaining. Maybe it was time to end this partnership.

His hand went to the sidearm on his hip as Juice swung up into the saddle. A gunshot would alert Lucian. Also, Blade might need both of them if Lucian put up a fight. He groaned under his breath as he reminded himself that both Juice and Ricki had waited for him to get out of the joint after they'd both been released from prison.

Still, he couldn't help being irritable. They'd been following the outfitter and the woman but had lost them yesterday afternoon. He removed his hand from his gun to swat at the swarm of mosquitoes buzzing around him.

"Let's go get Lucian and what he owes us and then get the hell out of this country."

They hadn't gone far when Blade smelled a campfire. He rode toward the scent along the trail that had them headed north—instead of higher up the mountain. He saw his two companions perk up as the scent of frying bacon and coffee became stronger.

A few minutes later, they cleared the pines to see a large camp with several big wall tents and a couple of smaller tents next to a creek. But as they reined in, he saw only one person.

"Calhoun St. Pierre around?" Blade asked the wrangler making breakfast over an open fire.

"He's with another client, different trip," the wrangler said.

"Do you know where they're headed?" he asked, convinced they were headed for the same place.

The wrangler shook his head.

"How about Lucian Beck's camp. We're going up there to meet him, but I think we got turned around."

For a moment, the wrangler looked as if he were going to deny knowing where the camp might be. "Nope, you're still on the right trail. I don't know exactly where it is. Just that it's up there." He pointed to the peak in the distance—that matched the description the biker had given them.

"So, you haven't seen St. Pierre and his client?"

When the wrangler shook his head, turning his attention to his cooking, Blade was pretty sure the man was lying. But he let it go when four fisherman came out of one of the larger tents to see what was going on.

"Maybe we'll cross paths," Blade suggested.

"Doubtful," the wrangler said with a laugh. "Not unless you get lost, since they aren't headed in the same direction you are."

Maybe, Blade thought, remembering how they'd lost their trail yesterday. He couldn't help being suspicious. If the outfitter had taken the client Blade heard he had up here, then they were both looking for Lucian.

"Thanks for your help," he said to the wrangler. No matter what the cowboy said, Blade had a feeling he'd be seeing St. Pierre and Lucian's wife soon.

GENEVA FELT AS if she had blisters on her legs and behind. She shifted in the saddle, glad that Calhoun had the puppy. They'd ridden back into the mountains for a couple of hours already. Just when she thought she couldn't take another minute of the pain, they reached the top of a ridge and small open area, and he drew his horse up.

She saw what was left of a lean-to, as Calhoun had called it. Basically, it was a couple of long poles attached to adjacent trees. The old tarp that had once formed a shelter across the top was in tatters. "Is this it?" she asked, glad to be off the saddle as she walked past the packhorses toward Calhoun.

He'd dismounted and was now inspecting the camp in the towering pines. She stopped next to his horse, watching him as he searched for tracks. If this was Lucian's camp, he obviously wasn't here. Had he been? Or was all of this a waste of time and energy? She tried to see him here and couldn't. Not the man she'd met and married.

Turning, she looked back at the way they'd come. The view was incredible. She realized how far she'd come from the life she'd known with Lucian. If he hadn't destroyed that life, she would never have made this journey. She breathed in the air, turning her face up into the sun and closing her eyes. It felt so good to be off the horse. She reminded herself that she still had to ride all the way back down again. *Thanks, Lucian.*

Strange, but she didn't feel that molten pit of anger she had on the long days driving up here in his pickup. She felt almost at peace until she looked at Calhoun, who was frowning. "What?" she demanded. "This is Lucian's camp, right?"

"No."

"No?"

"It's on up the mountain."

His answer seemed to zap all her strength. She sat down on the nearest fallen tree and stretched out her legs. Had they really come all this way, and they still weren't there? Turning her face up to the sun, she closed her eyes, but not even the morning rays and the high mountain air helped right now. She heard rather than saw Calhoun approach.

"Are you all right?" he asked quietly.

She didn't open her eyes because she might start crying. The sun felt heavenly on her face. She wasn't on a horse. She told herself that she didn't want anything or anyone to spoil this moment not in a saddle—especially Calhoun St. Pierre. "I see why you like it up here."

There was a smile in his voice when he spoke. "Some places just call a person."

She opened her eyes and looked at him. He'd hunkered down next to her and was looking out at the seemingly endless mountains ranges before them. She'd never felt a place call to her. She hadn't been called to where she lived in California; she'd been born there, raised there and still lived there. She'd left for trips but had never thought of moving. But now, she couldn't imagine what had kept her anchored to one place for so long.

"Has Lucian even been here?" she asked.

"Someone has. One person traveling with an extra horse. I can't tell if it was him. Maybe. I can see where the person made a small fire and hobbled the horses."

She opened her eyes to look at him. "He already left?" So why wasn't he more upset? Why wasn't she?

Worse, why was a part of her glad that they'd missed him? She'd been all about facing him, knowing she'd probably never see a cent of her money, but wanting to at least tell him what she thought of him. Right now, she couldn't have cared less. She was too tired and sore.

Her puppy came over and climbed into her lap. She found herself smiling as she looked down at her. The dog was growing, the little chubby legs getting longer and stronger every day.

"If it was Lucian, he didn't stay here long," Calhoun said, pushing to his feet. "He's headed for his high camp farther up. I'm going to take a look around, and then we need to go." With that, he walked off, all long legs and purpose, the puppy jumping off her lap to chase after him.

They were getting out of here to go to Lucian's high

camp farther up this mountain? She rose on shaky legs, groaning silently at the pain. "What if he just stepped away for a little while?" She called into the pines where Calhoun had disappeared to suggest the possibility but got no answer.

She listened but heard nothing. What if Calhoun ran into him out in the woods? Or worse, ran into the three men who he'd said had been following them yesterday? What if he didn't come back?

She looked around, feeling more alone than she ever had in her life. With Calhoun close by, she'd felt secure, safe and protected. But now she couldn't hear Calhoun or the puppy bustling through the trees. All she could hear was the wind high in the pine boughs, its sigh almost human. She felt a chill even though the sun was warm on her face. Would she even know how to get out of these mountains by herself? Remembering what Calhoun had said about her needing to know how to saddle up without him didn't help her growing concern.

A twig cracked somewhere in the distance. A squirrel began to chatter closer. Spotting Calhoun's rifle in the scabbard on his horse, she quickly moved to it and pulled it free. She assumed the weapon was loaded. She also assumed she wouldn't have to actually use it if anyone other than Calhoun came out of those trees.

"Put down the rifle."

She swung around, heart lodged in her throat. Calhoun stood in the clearing, the puppy in his arms. "Put down my dog."

Calhoun slowly lowered the puppy to the ground. "What are you doing?"

What *was* she doing? "I got scared."

He nodded as he walked toward her. "You know how to fire that?"

"I was hoping I wouldn't have to."

As he reached her, he grabbed the barrel of the gun and wrenched it from her hands. "Never point a gun at someone unless you're planning to use it. So let me show you how for next time." Next time? She watched as he patiently showed her how to load it and make sure it was ready to fire.

Her heart was pounding even as she told herself she'd never have to fire the rifle. At least she hoped not. "You could use some target practice, but that would alert anyone interested in us as to where we are. So, if you have to use it, point the sight on the end at the center of the person, take a breath, hold it and pull the trigger. Now, we need to get going." Again he didn't move, his gaze intent on her. Could he tell how terrified she was at the thought of shooting someone? He was right. She wasn't strong enough for this.

Calhoun was standing just inches from her. He smelled of pine and the outdoors. He looked so capable, easily shifting his tone from gentle with the puppy and her to fierce and scary with others when necessary.

When he spoke, his voice was soft. "Can you ride a little farther?"

She nodded, although it was the last thing she wanted to do.

"Then let's go. Come here, pup," he called to the dog. "You really need to give this dog a name. If you don't, I will." Their gazes met. She could feel the power of this man in the intensity of his gaze, she glimpsed a hunger in those eyes that matched her own and felt a shudder move through her. "Damn it, woman."

"That's a terrible name for a puppy," she whispered as he advanced on her.

He grabbed her, wrapping his free arm around her waist and pulled her hard into the solid wall of his chest. His mouth dropped to hers, forcing her head back as he pulled her even closer. Her lips parted as he deepened the kiss, opening her up with his tongue as she surrendered to his passion.

Geneva didn't hear the approaching riders. It was as if all her senses were on his plundering kiss and the rock-solid feel of his body against hers.

He drew back so quickly that she almost fell. Quickly moving away from her, he swung the rifle up into his hands and whispered for her to get the puppy and go into the pines and stay there. She scooped up the dog and, on trembling legs, plunged into the pines to drop behind a huge fallen tree.

A few moments later, two men rode into the camp.

Chapter Twelve

Geneva stayed crouched down where she was. Calhoun's voice floated on the air. She could only make out a few words of the conversation, but it was clear that he knew the men.

"Thanks for letting me know," she heard him say, and listened as the two men rode off before she stood and walked back into the clearing.

Calhoun was putting his rifle into his scabbard on his horse when she came out of the woods. She caught a glimpse of two riders through the pines before they disappeared from view.

"Who were those men?" she asked, sounding breathless from the kiss right before the surprise of horseback riders approaching.

He didn't answer right away. Nothing new there. She still had the taste of him on her lips, or she would have thought she'd dreamed the kiss. "Who were those men?" she asked again.

He stopped what he was doing, let out a sigh and turned. "They work for me. They rode over to tell me about the three men who came through their camp this morning. Now, could we please get moving?" He didn't wait for an answer as he took the puppy from her and swung up into the saddle.

"I guess this means we aren't going to talk about the kiss," she said as she started to walk back to her horse. She smiled to herself as she heard him swear under his breath. She'd gotten under his skin in more ways than one.

But then he'd done the same to her.

As she led her horse over to a stump, she mounted it as if she'd done this a million times. Her body felt as if she had. She touched her tongue to her upper lip, remembering the kiss, remembering the urgency in him as he'd pulled her against him. His arm had locked her in place with a strength that had made her dizzy. That woman he'd kissed and who'd kissed him back felt as if it had been someone else. She barely remembered that *other* Geneva Carrington Beck, the one who was still married to Lucian.

Once in the saddle and trailing up the mountain behind Calhoun, she looked at his broad back astride the horse and warned herself to be careful. She'd never met a man like this one. He wasn't the kind of man a woman dallied with, she told herself. That kiss proved it.

As she rode after him and the packhorses, she realized that whatever his men had told him, it had the outfitter worried and moving faster than he had before.

As CALHOUN GLANCED up toward the mountain ahead, he felt a chill. His men had brought him disturbing news, which he hadn't shared with Geneva. He'd wanted time to think, to make sure he wasn't going off half-cocked before he decided what to do. But he also had to get up this mountain as quickly as possible. Those three men who'd come through his outfitter camp this morning were on the other side of the mountain—not that far away.

Also, there was now no doubt that they were looking for the same thing he was—Lucian Beck. What the wranglers had told him about the three men had been the most disturbing of all. The one who'd done all the talking had a Southern accent and numerous prison tattoos. The others looked of the same ilk. Dangerous men on a dangerous mission. All noticeably armed and apparently determined to get to Lucian's camp.

All looking for Lucian. Or maybe something else. What bothered Calhoun is what they were all doing here looking for Lucian. Why did they think he was here? And if he was, why now? It had been over a year since he'd gone up into the mountains by himself, acting nervous, suspicious, before he'd taken off without saying goodbye. Unless Lucian stopping by and sleeping with Calhoun's fiancée was his idea of saying goodbye.

What really bothered him, though, was that, for some reason, Geneva wasn't the only one who thought Lucian had come back here. The question had always been, Why would Lucian show his face around Cooke City after the mess he'd left more than a year ago?

One reason kept coming up. Because he'd hidden something up here on this mountain, and now he'd come back for it. Geneva had hinted at the possibility. Calhoun had thought she was just clutching at straws in her hopes that she would find Lucian here.

But it would seem that the men after Lucian might be thinking the same thing. Calhoun couldn't see them making this trek up here unless there was more of a payoff than them just settling some old score with Lucian.

What worried him was that it might be the same reason Geneva had insisted on coming up here and putting herself through this arduous trip.

Any way Calhoun looked at it, trouble was headed right for them and right now. He wasn't sure who he could trust. He thought of Geneva pointing his rifle at him. She could have shot him if she'd wanted to. What did he know about her motives for wanting to come up here? He knew nothing about this woman other than what she'd told him, which hadn't been much.

Mentally, he kicked himself. What had he been thinking kissing her? He'd wanted to do a whole lot more than that, which worried him. Was this about Lucian? Or had this woman gotten to him?

He shook off the thought and tried to think clearly. From what his men had told him, the three weren't just armed, rough-looking and determined to get to Lucian's camp. One of them had a small collapsible shovel tied to his saddle. For a grave? Or something else?

The fact that the men had an idea where to find Lucian's camp meant that someone in Cooke City had to have told them. Which, given how few people even knew of the camp, Calhoun could narrow it down to one person. Biker William "Ace" Graham knew because he and Lucian had been tight when they were younger.

Calhoun wondered what it had taken for Ace to give up where those men might find Lucian though. He worried that Ace might not still be alive given what his wranglers had told him about the men after Lucian.

Thanks to his wranglers, the three outlaws were headed for Lucian's camp on the longer route around

the mountain. With luck, they would reach there after
he and Geneva had left.

But then what? Any fool would be able to follow his
and Geneva's trail now that the rain had stopped. Even if
the three missed them at Lucian's camp, Calhoun knew
the men could find them before they got off this mountain. So why was he still headed for Lucian's camp?

There was only one reason. If Lucian was there, Calhoun might have time to warn his old friend—not for
Lucian's sake but for his wife's. She thought she wanted
justice, but he suspected she was still in love with the man.
The problem was, even if Lucian was there, they might
not have time to warn him and then clear out before all
hell broke loose when the three outlaws showed up.

Calhoun reminded himself that this wasn't his fight.
He'd once owed Lucian his life, but that payment was
settled before Lucian slept with Calhoun's fiancée. He'd
felt no guilt for that until Geneva had shown up and now,
realizing that if he didn't try to warn Lucian, he would
be letting those men kill him.

The smart option was turning back, walking away
from a fight he couldn't win and wasn't his battle in any
case. No matter what he might feel for his old friend or
this woman who'd grudgingly earned his respect, he
didn't owe Lucian his life. Geneva especially didn't deserve this after what Lucian had already done to her.

Calhoun swore under his breath. So why was he trying to beat the men to the camp? To warn his once good
friend? Surely he didn't think that he could prevent whatever these men had planned for Lucian once they found
him. If not on this mountain, then these men would eventually find him. That kind of trouble would eventually

catch up with his old friend—and anyone who got in their way.

He felt a sliver of fear bury itself under his skin. Geneva Beck thought she wanted justice. He doubted she would like what she found—whether Lucian was up there or not. If Lucian was, he'd be lucky to get out of these mountains alive. But now Lucian wasn't the only one.

He realized he was avoiding what was really at stake here. The reason all of them were risking their lives.

Calhoun reined in his horse, dismounted and set down the puppy, who'd been sleeping curled in his lap. The sun lolled in a pristine blue sky overhead. The heat felt good, the smell of pine and creek water filling the high mountain air as he walked back to Lucian's wife, the dog on his heels. This had always been the place that had filled his soul.

Why had he brought Geneva up here? Because he'd thought she would be safer with him than Max. He still would be here now, he thought. He would have gone looking for Lucian without her. True, he shouldn't have kissed her, but he didn't regret it—especially if there was a good chance he might die today.

Admittedly, he'd expected her to give up by now and turn back. He'd planned on it, had it all mapped out, how he would take her over to the main camp and have one of the wranglers return her to town.

But once they crossed this next ridge, they would be in sight of Lucian's camp, and there would be no turning back for either of them. This was between him and his old friend. Geneva didn't realize it yet, but she didn't want any part of what would go down. They'd lost the men trailing them yesterday, but the men knew where he and Geneva were headed. They might even think they were after the same thing.

But what was that? The more Calhoun had thought about it, he knew that the three men were after more than vengeance against Lucian. He hadn't taken it seriously when Geneva had thrown out the idea of Lucian having hidden something back up here that he'd returned to retrieve. Given the interest in the three outlaws headed for Lucian's camp, he had a bad feeling he was the only one who didn't know what was really going on.

But he was about to find out, he thought as he and the puppy trailing after him reached Geneva. She seemed surprised that they had stopped.

"We need to talk," he said as he dragged her off her horse.

"WHAT ARE WE really doing up here?" Calhoun demanded, his fingers gripping her upper arms as he held her just inches from him.

Geneva couldn't have been more shocked by this change in him. She'd seen him angry, but this was different. She'd seen him gentle and almost sweet. She'd kissed this man. But right now, he was scaring her. "I don't know what you mean."

"I think you do. Why would Lucian come back here, let alone go up to his camp? It doesn't make any sense unless, like you said, he'd left something here that he'd come back for. What is it?" She opened her mouth, but nothing came out. His gaze hardened. "You haven't been completely honest with me, but you're going to right now. Tell me."

Geneva thought of Mitzi's blackmail threat to Lucian. So, maybe the two of them really hadn't been lovers. Not that it mattered anymore. She still couldn't be sure that Lucian and Mitzi hadn't been in on taking her for everything from the very beginning. What had made her angry was that she wasn't the one who'd found out Lucian's secret. She was just the naive, trusting woman who'd married him, believing everything he told her.

Calhoun gave her a little shake. "What aren't you telling me?"

"It has nothing to do with any of this," she said lifting her chin in defiance. "Why should you care about my reasons for wanting to go after Lucian?"

"Because my wranglers told me about the three men who had been following us. They're headed to the same place we are. They want Lucian. But I suspect they're after something more, and you know what it is, and we're not going another foot until you tell me."

She looked down at where her engagement and wedding ring had been. She could no longer see the pale imprint where they'd been. Gone as if it had never been there.

"Don't lie to me," Calhoun said in a low growl.

Lucian's betrayal had been enough. She didn't want to tell this man about her best friend's as well. But when she looked into his eyes, she saw something else behind the anger.

"Why did you really bring me up here?" she demanded. He let go of her, drawing back as if in surprise. "You broke your own rule about women. On top of that, you had every reason not to help me given what Lucian had done to you. So, what are we really doing here?"

Surprise gave way to anger that seemed more directed

at himself than her now. "That's what I'm telling you. I wish I hadn't. These men who are after Lucian, they will kill us and him too if I'm right and there is more to this than just getting closure from your husband. Who are these men and what do they want? Time is running out. Tell me."

Geneva swallowed. "You didn't tell me why you brought me up here. *Don't lie to me*."

He actually smiled at his words being thrown back at him. Shaking his head, he said, "Were you always like this?"

"No. I'm terrified of this woman Lucian has made me into."

Calhoun nodded as if she scared him too. "Just tell me this, whatever it is Lucian's neck deep in, were you in on it with him?"

She looked him in the eye. "No. I swear. He blindsided me. If he hadn't forgotten the key to the storage shed…"

"That's where you found the pickup and the photos?"

Geneva hesitated, but only for a moment. He was right. It was time to be completely honest. He needed to know the truth. "There was also a note to Lucian written by someone I considered my best friend," she said. "Lucian didn't leave alone."

"He took off with your best friend?" Calhoun swore, then his eyes narrowed as if realizing that wasn't why they were up here on this mountain.

"I don't know if they were romantically involved or not. I'm pretty sure the note I found was a blackmail threat. Apparently, my friend Mitzi recognized my engagement and wedding ring set as one that was stolen in a jewelry store robbery in Alabama. The four masked thieves were caught on video but never captured—nor was the one-of-a-kind jewelry worth over several million dollars ever found. The notice had been posted in a pawn shop Mitzi frequents when she needs money. Her husband keeps her on a short chain financially. Or at least he did before she took everything she could scrape up and left him as well."

"When was this robbery?" Calhoun demanded.

"Days before the last time you said you saw Lucian in Cooke City," she said.

CALHOUN CLOSED HIS eyes for a moment, everything starting to make sense. Lucian's behavior the last time he saw him. His friend going up to his camp alone. Maybe even him sleeping with Dana. Lucian had been on the run after probably double-crossing the men who'd helped him with the theft of the jewelry.

He looked at the woman standing before him. Betrayed by her husband and her best friend. That would make anyone want to avenge herself. But still he had to ask. "I'm guessing that Lucian ripped off his partners in crime and came back to Montana to hide his ill-gotten gains until the heat died down. So, where do you fit into all of this?"

She shook her head. "I have no idea. I guess he was just killing time until he could get the jewelry and realized he could make enough off me to carry out his plan with my money until he could fence the jewelry or whatever he has planned."

"What I don't understand is why now? If he has all your money, why not forget about the stolen jewelry he hid?"

"Greed? Or maybe married to me, he was hidden from his past. But once he surfaced and started throwing money around, there were other people after him. Several stopped by the house looking for him before I left San Diego."

Did it really matter? This woman wasn't the only one who thought Lucian had come back here. But at least now he knew why. "I've never understood why you wanted to come up here looking for him. Are you sure this isn't about the stolen jewelry?"

Her laugh was brittle with bitterness. "I didn't even know about the jewelry theft until when I discovered the blackmail note from my best friend to my husband hidden with some other papers in the glove box of the pickup. I know it must seem ridiculous to you that I want to face Lucian, look him in the eye and tell him what he did to me."

"Not so ridiculous."

A thought seemed to cross her mind. She eyed him suspiciously. "You really didn't know about it? Lucian didn't tell you about the jewelry heist?"

He let out a string of oaths. "You think I wouldn't have turned him in?"

"I don't know. Had he slept with your fiancée yet?"

Calhoun chuckled. "Good point, but I can tell you one thing. I wouldn't have brought you up here if I'd known."

"But you still would have come."

She knew he would have. That should have bothered him more than it did. While he'd been trying to figure out this woman, she'd been doing the same with him. He rubbed his neck for a moment. He had to decide what to do. Either way, they had to get moving.

He feared it might already be too late to abort. The

three outlaws would be traveling fast once they got what they'd come up into these mountains for. Once they'd dealt with Lucian. If they found him but not the jewelry, they might get it into their heads that he and Geneva knew more than they did. After all, they seemed to be after the same thing—both headed for Lucian's camp.

He weighed their options quickly, knowing that time was of the essence. What if they got to Lucian's high camp and he'd already come and gone? What would the men after him do then? He and Geneva would be sitting ducks—especially if they turned around now and headed back to town. The men might think that they had the goods.

They couldn't win for losing, he thought, wishing he could get his hands on Lucian for doing this, not just to him but to Geneva. He wanted to blame her for them being in this spot, but he knew it was his own fault. He'd wanted to protect her and give her closure. But he also wanted it for himself. If Lucian was at his high camp, Calhoun had a few scores of his own he wanted to settle with him.

But that meant getting to the camp before the three men did.

He looked at Geneva. This morning her blue eyes were the exact color of Montana's summer sky. The memory of the kiss made his knees weak. Worse, he wasn't sure he would be able to protect her. The odds weren't good. She had to know what they were up against. This wasn't a decision he could make on his own.

"We're between a rock and a hard place," he said. "Your husband is in a world of trouble. He's ripped off the wrong people. He's probably about to get what he deserves. Quite frankly, I don't think he's worth dying for."

GENEVA SAW IT coming even before he said the words.

"I'm going to take you over to my camp so one of my wranglers can get you back to town. Once there, you can pick up the truck and drive out as quickly as you can."

"Don't I have any say in this?"

He met her gaze. "Haven't you made enough bad decisions lately? What are you doing out here in the wilds with a man you don't even know?"

"I don't think you're that scary."

He laughed at that, shaking his head, before his gaze found hers again. "I hate to mention that you might not be the best judge of men."

"You're not like Lucian."

"I might be worse," he said stepping closer. "You think I haven't thought about settling one old score with my former friend by sleeping with his *wife* the way he slept with my fiancée?" His gray eyes bored into hers. "You have no idea how tempting it is."

"Don't I?"

"Be careful," he whispered, leaning even closer. "There are some impulsive decisions you can't take back."

"Like you sending me back to town while you go on up to Lucian's camp alone?" she asked, standing her ground.

"I don't want to get you killed. Is that so hard to understand?"

"You said yourself there isn't time for you to take me to your camp and then reach Lucian's before the men after him get there. You'd be walking into an ambush."

She shook her head. "If Lucian's up there, someone has to warn him."

Calhoun swore. "You sure about that?"

She gave him an impatient look. "You didn't have to bring me up here. You wanted to settle some things with Lucian as much as I did."

"Fair enough, but now that I know what's at stake, I can't take you to his camp. I won't risk your life. We'll both turn back. I'll take you to town myself."

"How far is Lucian's camp?"

He thought about lying. "Just over the next rise."

"You would make better time alone without me and the packhorses," she said. "Leave me here. Go warn Lucian, then come back."

He stared at her. "You still love him."

"I still love the man I thought I married," she said. "But that man never existed. Can you live with yourself if you don't go warn him? That's what I thought. Go, I'll be all right. I've watched you care for the horses. I can do it." She could feel his gaze measuring her as she picked up her puppy, who'd been playing in the wildflowers at their feet.

Calhoun met her gaze again before he reached down into his boot and pulled out a handgun. "It's point and shoot once you pull this back." He handed it to her, showing her how to hold it in both of her hands, to steady it, to point at her target, put the red dot on the spot, take a breath, hold it and then press the trigger.

"Remember, if you point it at someone, you'd better be ready to shoot." He hesitated. She could see the battle going on inside him. "I don't like leaving you here alone. I'm going to leave my horse and go on foot up to the camp."

Her hand shook as she tucked the gun into the vest pocket. She was no longer in the world she'd grown up in. She felt as if she'd traveled to a foreign land where there were no rules except survival by any means.

She'd known this country up here in the mountains was dangerous. Men carried guns to protect themselves from the wild animals—but apparently also from each other. They knew that once they left the paved roads, they were on their own. Capable men like Calhoun St. Pierre who felt at home up here and yet respected the danger because it was always here.

"You'll be back for me."

"And if I'm not?" he asked holding her gaze.

She smiled at that. "You'll be back."

He handed her what he said was a satellite phone. "If I don't come back, call for help."

CALHOUN HATED LEAVING HER. He wouldn't be able to protect her if he took her with him. He sure as hell wouldn't be able to protect her leaving her alone back there either.

But the truth was that she'd been in danger the moment she met Lucian Beck. If the men after her husband didn't get what they wanted, they would be coming after her. If not on this mountain, then when she returned home. There would be no escaping the hole Lucian had dug for himself—and her.

She was already in jeopardy. Leaving her even for the time it would take to get to Lucian's camp and back, made him more than nervous. He felt as if he'd been left few options. Taking her with him was far more dangerous because, unlike her, he didn't trust Lucian not to kill them both.

Lucian's camp was just over the rise, much closer than he'd wanted Geneva to know. He could feel the three men breathing down his neck. They would be moving fast. They would want this over quickly. They'd taken a longer route, but they too would be anxious to get to Lucian, to get to the jewelry before he absconded with it. With luck Calhoun would beat them to the camp. If Lucian was there...

He realized that all of this might be for nothing. Lucian could be miles from here. He could already be in another country.

Except that Calhoun didn't believe that. Once he'd heard about the jewelry heist, he knew that Lucian had come back for the loot. Once he had it, he would be gone, leaving the rest of them to deal with the men after him. Leaving Geneva in trouble. It wouldn't take long for the men to find out that she was Lucian's wife once they returned to Cooke City empty-handed. But only if they didn't already know who she was.

That was why Calhoun was making his way up the side of the mountain toward the rim of rock to Lucian's high camp. Not to warn his former friend but to make sure the three men got what they'd come up this mountain for. He planned to end this for Geneva, because she deserved better.

Chapter Thirteen

Calhoun worked his way through the trees. The only sound was the breeze in the branches, but he wasn't fooled. Lucian would have heard him coming. He might have been expecting him. The two of them had spent a lot of years in these mountains. He doubted his old friend would have lost his instincts for survival up here.

The camp sat high on the side of the mountain, butted against a sheer rock cliff and hidden from view by a large boulder. The mountain was steep, but there was a flat spot high on the cliff behind the huge rock. Lucian had stumbled on this spot when they were young, scrambling up the steep mountain to climb the boulder. He'd wanted to see the view from the top of it.

Calhoun thought of him with his arms spread wide, a grin just as broad on his face as he stood there precariously balanced on the top of the boulder. A fall would have killed him. That was Lucian. It wasn't until Calhoun joined him that he saw Lucian was right. It was the perfect place for a camp. A flat space for a lean-to hidden by rocks miles from civilization. The camp was just hard enough to get to.

From that point on, it had been Lucian's high camp, although the two of them had spent many hours up here hunting elk and fishing the high mountain lakes on the other side of it. The view had been amazing, which meant that if Lucian was up here, he might have already spotted him coming up the mountain.

Calhoun battled the memories as he circled around and came in the side of the camp. He wondered which of them had failed the other as longtime friends. He had to admit that he'd lost track of Lucian after college. He hadn't tried to find him, but then Lucian hadn't reached out to him—and Calhoun had been a whole lot easier to find.

He spotted the tracks first. They were fresh. He could see where someone had dug into the dirt at the base of the cliff. He moved to it, not surprised to find a good-sized empty hole. Lucian had been here and retrieved what he'd come back to Montana for.

Checking the rest of the small flat area, he saw tracks where one man had led two horses down the backside of the mountain because it wasn't as steep. That's when he saw that something had been scratched into the large boulder at eye level. It took him a moment to make out the crudely written words.

Sorry I missed you old buddy

Calhoun swore as he stepped to the edge of the mountain and looked out past the top of the huge boulder. Lucian hadn't just been here. He'd known they were behind him, coming for him. He must have spotted them.

But did he know about the three outlaws also coming for him? They would be riding up from the backside of his camp. They might have already found him.

His heart pounded as he started to hurry back to the

steep trail he'd come up. If the men hadn't found him, then Lucian might be headed down the mountain. He might stumble across Geneva. Lucian couldn't be that far ahead of him. In fact...

He realized his mistake too late. He heard the rumble of moving rocks. He didn't bother to look behind him at the cliff, he knew at once that Lucian hadn't really left, just as he knew what Lucian had done.

Calhoun threw himself down the mountain, running for his life as the landslide behind him began to careen down, crashing into the pines next to him. Calhoun was fast on his feet, but not fast enough to beat an avalanche of rock.

It roared down, stones bouncing all around him as he scrambled for shelter below the massive boulder. One rock struck his leg, another his shoulder. But it was the one that hit him in the side of the head that turned out the lights as he crashed into a pile of dried pine needles.

GENEVA TOOK CARE of the horses, then got something for her and the puppy to eat. The sun beat down on her, forcing her into the shade. She could feel time slipping away and tried not to worry about Calhoun.

He would come back for her. She had to believe that. But what would he find when he reached Lucian's camp? There was already bad blood between him and his former friend. That she had no idea what would happen when the two met again worried her. She didn't have any idea how her husband would react to seeing Calhoun up here—let alone finding out that he'd brought her.

It just made her more aware of how little she'd known

Lucian. Look what he'd done to her. What would he do to Calhoun? Or his former friend to him?

She started at a rumbling sound off in the distance and stopped to listen. More thunder? Another storm. It sounded close but ended fairly quickly. She hugged herself against the chill that raced over her flesh. She told herself that Calhoun would be back soon. Her phone was in her bag, but without being able to charge it, even if she could get cell service up here, there was no reason to check it.

Calhoun had left her a gun, food, shelter and a satellite phone to use if he didn't come back. What he hadn't said was that if she got into trouble, no one would be coming to help her in time. She was on her own for the first time in her life in a place that was frightening even without possible killers headed this way.

But to her surprise, she wasn't terrified—not the way she'd been when she'd realized that Lucian had left her and taken all of her money and dignity. That had been a different kind of fear, a different kind of alone. She'd never felt that kind of desperation before.

That she felt stronger surprised her as well. She breathed in the day, listening to the breeze swaying the pine boughs over her head. A kind of peace filled her. From the moment she'd awakened alone after her anniversary party, she'd been consumed with finding Lucian and—what? Making him pay?

Now she wasn't sure what she needed from him. A divorce would be nice. But other than that, she didn't expect much of anything. She was sure that Calhoun was right, and the money was gone. The puppy came over and licked her hand before falling over on her back in the grass and biting at a blue flower bobbing above her head.

Geneva smiled, thankful for the dog. She'd questioned why Lucian had given her such a present. Because he'd known it would make their friends ooh and aah over it. Make people think he was the best husband ever. It made no sense, considering that the next day, everyone would know the truth.

She rubbed the puppy's pink belly, wanting to see this gift as a sign that Lucian wasn't all bad. That maybe a part of him had loved her. That the only reason he'd left was because he was desperate. That it hadn't been easy to walk away from her.

Then she noticed the faint line from the small scratch on her wrist where her watch had been and feared she was wrong. Was that why she wanted to come face-to-face with her husband? To find out the truth about him?

At a sound off in the trees, both she and the puppy froze. Unlike the rumbling sound she'd heard earlier, this one was much closer. She held her breath, waiting to hear it again. Her hand went to the gun in her vest pocket as she scooped up the dog with her free hand and moved to a spot in full sun, feeling a chill.

Had she and the puppy heard Calhoun returning? She tried to measure how much time had passed by the angle of the sun. Maybe it was Calhoun back already. He'd gone to the campsite, hadn't found Lucian and was now back. At least she hoped it was him.

One of the horses let out a whinny. She heard a rustling sound in the opposite direction at the same time the puppy barked, making her jump. She swung around, leading with the gun as a man stepped out of the woods.

Chapter Fourteen

"Lucian." Geneva stared at the man who walked out of the pines toward her. It was just shy of a week since he'd left her, and yet she barely recognized him. He hadn't shaved, his beard scruffy, and his hair, usually always neat with the products he used, was now ruffled in the breeze.

He was dressed much like Calhoun, same type of canvas pants and long-sleeved knit shirt under fleece. He wore cowboy boots, apparently an old pair he'd had hidden somewhere, since they didn't look new.

He also had a gun strapped to his hip. She didn't doubt that it was loaded, and he knew how to shoot it. No wonder she barely recognized him. Even his expression wasn't one she'd seen before. She didn't know this man. No doubt ever had.

He stopped a half dozen yards from her. "What are you doing here?" he asked, his words heavy with what could have been regret. Or anger.

"I found your pickup, your photos and the note from Mitzi," she said hugging the puppy closer. The gun was still in her hand but pointed at the ground. She didn't remember doing that. It was as if seeing Lucian had made her forget that she had the weapon. "Everything I found led me here."

"To Calhoun." He nodded, smiling almost wistfully. "You always were smarter than me, though I never expected this."

It confirmed what she'd suspected. "So, you didn't leave it for me to find you," she said, disappointed because she'd wanted to believe he'd had some remorse. That he'd left it to give her a chance to—if nothing else—tell him what she thought of him.

"No," he said with a shake of his head. "I wanted to spare you from ever having to see me again."

"How gallant of you."

Lucian looked at the ground. "Go ahead. Tell me what a bastard I am. I deserve it."

She had thought it was something she wanted, but looking at him, she no longer cared. "I assume you've spent all my money."

"Our money," he corrected. "Sorry, but I owed a lot of people who wanted to kill me."

"I can understand the feeling. Why?" she asked. "Why would you marry me and then leave me like you did?"

He shrugged. "I already told you. I owed a lot of people who wanted to kill me."

"Was that your plan from the moment you met me?"

He gave her a sheepish look. "Pretty much."

"Was Mitzi in on it?"

"Not hardly. I know she's your friend, but she proved to be a pain in the neck. I couldn't wait to ditch her." He motioned to the gun in her hand. "You going to shoot me?"

"There are still a lot of people who want that pleasure—like the men on their way up here who think you have the jewelry from the robbery," she said.

He lifted a brow. "Right, so you know about that. The

note from Mitzi. I should never have given you those rings, but they were beautiful, and I wanted to impress your father."

"My father? Nice to know you were thinking of him and not me, although it's clear that I was just a mark to you. No surprise after the way things ended. At our anniversary party, no less. If I'm not mistaken, you drugged me and let everyone think I drank too much, right?"

"What can I say? I'm no good, but you've realized that by now," Lucian said. "If it helps, leaving you was one of the hardest things I've ever done. I would have stayed if there was any possible way. I liked the lifestyle you could afford me. But I owed too much money, had too many people looking for me, and I'm greedy. I didn't even want to share it with you."

"Why are you saying these things?"

"What? You don't want to hear the truth?" he asked. "I thought that's why you came up here."

She noticed the protective way he placed his hand over the saddle bag thrown over his shoulder. His other hand hung at his side. Next to the weapon holstered at his hip.

"What now?" she asked. "You fence the jewels, skip the country, buy that island you always wanted?"

"You don't want to know. You shouldn't have come up here."

"You're right. I'm sorry I did."

"Why did you?" He sounded as if he genuinely wanted to know.

"At first, it was about finding you. I wanted to face you, ask why. But at some point, I no longer cared. You're not the man I thought I married. You should get on down the mountain before the men who want to kill you catch up to you."

"I did one thing nice for you." He nodded toward the puppy in her arms. "What did you name her?"

The name came to her in that moment. The puppy had gotten her through the days and nights after Lucian left. It had made this journey with her. It had given her hope that she wouldn't always hurt the way she had at first. It had shown her even a side of Calhoun St. Pierre that she wouldn't have seen otherwise. She was Geneva's good luck charm.

"Her name's Lucky. She helped me get through this even if you were the one to give her to me."

He laughed, shaking his head. "You always did see a half empty glass and think it was almost full. You were just wrong about me."

She could see that. He lifted his head as if listening. Was he worried that Calhoun would show up at any moment? Or, she realized as her breath caught, her heart dropping, did he know something she didn't—that Calhoun was never coming back?

"Tell me you didn't do anything to Calhoun," she said, her voice breaking.

"Calhoun, is it?" Lucian swore. "I should have known he'd use you to pay me back."

She made a disgusted sound. "You think everyone is like you? Calhoun isn't like that. He went up the mountain to warn you about the men after you. That's the kind of friend he is."

Lucian laughed. "Boy, he sure showed you, but when it comes to men, you really aren't that experienced, are you?" His face sobered. He looked almost sad. "You should have stayed in California. I didn't want it to end like this. That's why I drugged you and left you on the couch. I never dreamed you'd come after me. By the way, where is my truck? I realized too late that I'd misplaced the storage unit key. I hope you didn't mess up my truck. I want it back."

That he wasn't worried about Calhoun answered her greatest fear. He had done something to him. The outfitter wouldn't be showing up here and saving her. She couldn't bear the thought that he might be dead or badly injured back up this mountain. She'd gotten Calhoun into this. He would have never been here if it wasn't for her.

"Some friend you turned out to be," she said, hating the way her voice broke.

"I made a worse husband," he said with a laugh. "Here's the problem, Geneva, we both know you aren't going to let me walk away. The minute you get back to town, you'll call the cops. You can see the problem we have here. I can't let you do that."

She told herself that he wouldn't hurt her, then realized the damage he'd already done to her. But could he kill her? She looked into his handsome face and saw a desperate stranger standing there.

Could she shoot this stranger with Lucian's face? She felt the weight of the weapon in her hand. She wasn't sure she could. The puppy kept wriggling. She couldn't hold on to her much longer since she'd gotten so heavy. She had to put her down on the ground, but as she did, she feared Lucian would take advantage of her movement and go for the weapon at his hip.

Instead, the moment the puppy's feet touched the ground, Lucian called the dog to him. Before she had time to realize her mistake, Lucky raced to him and Lucian snatched up the puppy, tucking her under his arm.

"I think you might have made a mistake naming this dog Lucky." His eyes narrowed as he looked across the space between them. "Throw down your gun, Geneva."

Chapter Fifteen

Calhoun woke in pain and covered with rocks and dirt. He pushed off the larger ones and tried to sit up. His head swam. For a moment, he couldn't remember what had happened. Then it came back in a rush. The rock-slide. Lucian.

He swore under his breath as he pushed himself up. One clear thought emerged through the pain. He had to get to Geneva before it was too late. Climbing over the rubble from the slide, he became aware of his injured leg and shoulder. Both hurt like hell, but nothing seemed to be broken, at least he hoped not. He had a hard head, thankfully. He didn't think he had a concussion. At least not a bad one.

He stumbled down the mountain, trying not to make too much noise for fear Lucian would hear him. He didn't know where his old friend was. Maybe he'd set off the rockslide, then gone another way out of the mountains. Or maybe right now he was with his wife.

Calhoun's fear pushed him harder even with his head feeling woozy and his shoulder and leg making every step filled with debilitating pain. Fortunately, he didn't have far to go. He moved down through the pines and over the ridge. All his instincts told him Geneva was all right. He hadn't heard a gunshot. But then again, he couldn't be sure she'd be able to pull the trigger if it was Lucian.

He didn't know how much time he'd been knocked out. He might not had have heard the gunshot. It might already be too late. He told himself that Lucian wouldn't kill her. Otherwise, Calhoun wouldn't have left her. He'd almost convinced himself that Lucian could have killed her while they were married and taken everything legally and hadn't.

But even as he thought it, he feared he was wrong. Lucian had never been patient. It was amazing that he'd waited this long to come back for the jewelry. Maybe even more amazing that he'd waited a year of marriage to leave Geneva, unless there was another reason he had to wait.

Even as a boy, his friend had wanted what he wanted when he wanted it. There was no waiting with Lucian, which was why he'd been a lousy elk hunter. He couldn't just sit and wait for a perfect shot. It was why he'd had to follow a blood trail for miles sometimes to find his elk and finally kill it.

Calhoun thought about Geneva—and the gun he'd left her. She wouldn't be able to kill Lucian, and that would be her last mistake when it came to the man. She still thought there was good in him. Was she still thinking that there was a chance Lucian could change? That they could be together?

The thought made him grind his teeth. He'd been drawn to her because of her strength—not her misplaced loyalty to the man who'd lied and cheated and left her. He'd seen her as a survivor. She hadn't curled up in a ball crying. She'd gotten in Lucian's pickup and come all the way to Cooke City after him.

On this whole arduous trip up the mountain, she hadn't complained or whined. She'd almost cried a couple of times, but she hadn't. She was strong and more capable than he'd ever suspected—more than even she herself had thought, he figured. Lucian hadn't broken her. Calhoun couldn't let him kill her.

But right now, he had no idea what she would do if Lucian found her. Tell him off? Beg him to come back to her? He shook his head. Whatever it was she needed from her lying, cheating, abandoning husband, Calhoun feared it was going to get her killed. Lucian might have already found her and not bothered to give her a chance to tell him how she felt about him, he thought as he caught a glimpse of the clearing where he'd left her.

BLADE COULD SEE at once that Lucian wasn't here as he rode into the camp. It was exactly as the biker had described it. But what a long ride to get here. He was sick of Ricki and Juice complaining and more than once had wanted to shoot the two of them.

Like his companions, he ached from riding the damned horse. Riding a horse had looked adventurous and exciting in movies. Instead, it was barbaric. Lucian would love putting him and the others through this agonizing experience. It would give him so much satisfaction—just as Blade was sure ripping them off after the heist had.

Dismounting, he couldn't ignore the pain in his legs as he followed the tracks in the still damp ground to the hole at the base of the cliffs where someone had dug.

He knew the jewelry wouldn't be there, but still he had to look. The boot tracks were fresh. Lucian's? Or had the space been empty when whoever this was had walked over to look?

When he'd met Lucian, he hadn't known about his connection to Montana or about this camp high in the mountains. He and his cohorts had come to realize how little Lucian had told them was even true. So much for honor among thieves.

But then again, they'd all met in prison. Probably not the best place to find people you could trust. The thing was, he'd liked Lucian, who appeared to be down on his luck after being arrested for domestic abuse and sentenced to a year in prison. He said his girlfriend had tried to kill him, and all he'd done was defend himself, and his girlfriend had gotten into a fight earlier in a bar brawl.

It was later, when they were all out, that Blade had run into Lucian. Not too surprising it was in a saloon. Lucian had told him that he and his new girlfriend had gotten into a fight. From the black eye and cut lip, Lucian had gotten the worst of it. What Blade had found interesting was that this girlfriend Lucian had been dating worked at a jewelry store.

He bought Lucian a beer. Later that evening, after plying him with liquor, Lucian said the reason they'd fought was because he'd found out about a big hush-hush shipment that was coming in next week. She'd been all cranky and on edge about it. He'd snooped on her phone, thinking she had a man on the side, and found out about the shipment. He wanted to take the entire shipment but said he had no idea how. At least that was his story.

That's where Blade and his little group of criminals

came in. Without them, Lucian would have never been able to pull off the heist. That's the part that kept Blade up at night planning his vengeance. He'd promised himself he would find Lucian and then make him pay.

What had surprised him was that the jewelry had never surfaced. He'd taken Lucian for an amateur. He'd thought for sure that the fool would try to pawn the jewelry or try to sell it to a fence who turned out to be an undercover cop. It seemed though that Lucian hadn't done either. Nor had he sold off a piece at a time like an amateur would have.

Blade had tried to find the woman who'd worked at the jewelry store, but she'd disappeared. The cops wanted her for questioning. It looked like a dead end, like Lucian was going to get away with what he'd done to them.

Blade had a friend in law enforcement, had given the cop Lucian's name and said he'd make it worth his while if he let him know if Lucian Beck ever turned up.

After a year, he'd almost given up hope. Then he'd gotten a call that Beck had been pulled over in Red Lodge, Montana, for speeding. It hadn't taken much for Blade to find out where Lucian had been headed. He had no idea what Lucian planned to do once he retrieved the jewelry wherever he'd hidden it, but he suspected someone in Cooke City would know where he could find his backstabbing cohort.

Blade had been surprised that Lucian had sat on the stolen jewelry all this time, waiting. But for what? He'd asked a few questions around Cooke City, Lucian's old stomping grounds. Once he'd learned about a camp up in the mountains, the pieces had begun to fall into place. He tracked the man through his illicit past to his old friend Calhoun St. Pierre. Unfortunately, the outfitter had already headed for the hills—with Lucian's woman.

Blade had no idea what Lucian had planned. It still wouldn't be easy to turn the jewelry into cash. But it was clear that someone had been here, and now that person had the jewelry. Lucian? Or Calhoun St. Pierre?

So, where is the jewelry now? he asked himself as he studied the tracks in the soft still damp earth.

"He's not here," Juice said. "Maybe he was killed in the rockslide."

"You think?" Blade headed back to his horse. "Maybe he started the rockslide. Sounds more like him. He can't be that far ahead of us. See the tracks? He's got what he came for and is heading out of these mountains. We're going to find him before that happens."

CALHOUN FOLLOWED LUCIAN'S tracks straight to Geneva. He tried to convince himself that his old friend wouldn't hurt her. He had to have felt something for her to marry her and wait a whole year before he left. But the truth was that Lucian had already hurt her.

Worse, Calhoun had left Geneva with a gun that he doubted she would be able to fire at her husband. He just hoped she didn't point it at Lucian, who might just be looking for an excuse to kill her. After all, his old friend had just left him for dead after starting a rockslide he assumed had killed him. It almost had. It wasn't like Lucian had come to check to see if he was still breathing.

He should have known he might be walking into a trap. He just hadn't expected Lucian to try to kill him. Just as Geneva wouldn't either. Calhoun had almost perished because he'd trusted his old friend. Geneva still loved the man. She didn't stand a chance against him.

As Calhoun neared the edge of the clearing, he pulled his weapon. He could hear voices, he realized with a wave of relief. Geneva was still alive. Should he race in guns blazing or try to sneak into camp? Lucian wouldn't be expecting him, thinking he was dead. But every moment he did nothing could cost Geneva her life.

It was a gamble, but one he had to take. He came out of the pines moving fast. He had no idea what he could find. The moment he cleared the pines, he saw something that made his heart drop. Geneva and Lucian in what appeared to be a standoff. In that split second, he saw Geneva, the gun in her hand, her gaze locked with Lucian's. Across from her, her husband held the puppy with one hand, his free hand going for the gun at his hip.

Chapter Sixteen

Geneva hadn't heard Calhoun approach. Her gaze was locked with Lucian's. Her only thought, fear for her puppy.

"Drop the gun, Geneva." Lucian's other hand moved as he went for his weapon. "I swear I'll kill—"

She pulled the trigger as Calhoun had instructed her, terrified that she would hit the puppy. But she couldn't bear watching him hurt Lucky. Her first shot must have been close because Lucian flinched. Her second was more accurate. She thought she heard a third shot but was sure she hadn't fired it.

Lucian dropped Lucky into the tall grass. Her gaze went to the dog, panicked that she might have hit her or the fall had hurt her. But to her relief, the puppy was on her chubby feet and headed in her direction through the grass.

That's when she looked up and saw that Lucian was gone. Not dead. Just…gone. And Calhoun… She hadn't seen him until after she'd fired the second shot. Until Lucian dropped the puppy and her attention had moved to Lucky as the puppy raced toward her.

She scooped the dog up into her arms as Calhoun rushed to her. "Are you hit?" he cried grabbing her shoulders and locking his gaze with hers.

She shook her head, unable to speak for a moment. "I thought you were dead." She began to cry as Calhoun hugged her and the dog. She looked past him. "Lucian?"

"He got away."

"I didn't kill him?" She remembered seeing Lucian stagger, thought she remembered seeing blood.

"No, you only wounded him."

She felt relieved. She didn't want to kill anyone. "He threatened to hurt Lucky." She looked down at the dog between them.

"Lucky?" Calhoun asked.

"You have to admit, she's one lucky dog." Her face fell. "Lucian was threatening to harm her."

"But you stopped him." He wasn't looking at the puppy. He was looking at her. It was a look she'd glimpsed before in his eyes. Admiration? She didn't feel that what she'd done was admirable in anyway. She could have killed a man. Not just any man, the man she'd married. It made her sick. She began to shake, her teeth chattering.

He pulled her closer. "He would have killed you if you hadn't pulled that trigger. He wouldn't have spared Lucky either."

She nodded, knowing it was true. Lucian had told her he couldn't let her go to the cops. He hadn't left the truck keys because he'd wanted her to come after him. He'd made a mistake. Just as she'd made a mistake when she'd married him and again when she'd come all the way to Montana, expecting some form of remorse from him for what he'd done to her.

Calhoun moved and she saw him wince.

"You're hurt," she cried.

"I'll live."

She saw the blood soaked into his hat. "Calhoun, what happened? Lucian…what did he do? He tried to hurt you, didn't he?"

"No, he tried to kill me. Just as he would have you if you hadn't shot him." He cupped her cheek in his warm hand. "Let's get out of here." He seemed to read her frightened look. "Lucian is headed down the mountain. We'll go to my camp to the northeast."

She realized how hard it must have been for him not to go after Lucian. "You're giving him a chance to get away," she said unable to hide her surprise.

"I wanted to go after him," he said. "But I'm not leaving you alone again. I almost got you killed, and those men after him are still somewhere on this mountain."

CALHOUN SAW THE effect of his words, but by now she had to know who and what they were dealing with. He had desperately wanted to chase Lucian down and end this once and for all, but it was true what he'd told Geneva. It would have meant leaving her alone again. He couldn't do that, even as hard as it was to let the bastard get away.

Those men after Lucian would find the camp empty and follow not only Lucian's tracks but also his own right to them.

"We can't stay here. Lucian left us to deal with his former partners in crime," Calhoun said. As long as Lucian had the jewelry, Geneva was in danger. They all were. He thought about using the satellite phone to call the authorities. But there was no law enforcement in Cooke City, none for miles. There were park rangers right over the border in Yellowstone National Park, but though some were trained just like law enforcement officers, their authority was inside the park—not outside the border.

Calhoun had wanted to end this up here on the mountain, but now that wasn't going to happen. He got the horses ready. He wondered how badly Lucian was injured. If his wound was life-threatening, he might not make it far. Geneva's second shot had wounded him, but Calhoun's had also.

As soon as they reached his camp with his wranglers there to protect Geneva, he would go looking for Lucian—even though it might mean running into the three outlaws also after him.

He saw Geneva carry the puppy over to the spot where Lucian had been standing. She held the dog against her chest as she looked down to where there was blood on the ground. Head wounds tended to bleed—even if the bullet had only grazed Lucian's scalp. The third shot, the one Calhoun had fired, had hit Lucian in the chest as he'd dropped the puppy. It was hard to say which wound would stop him—if either of them could.

"Let's go," he said, hating to see the pain on her face.

"I wanted to kill him."

"I understand," he said. She had no idea how much he understood or how hard pulling that trigger had been for her. He'd had experience with killing after serving for a time in Afghanistan. He had hoped never to have to fire a fatal shot at a man again. He especially hadn't wanted it to be at his former friend.

"I'm glad I didn't kill him."

"I understand that too," he said.

She handed him Lucky and headed for her horse but didn't get far before she stopped and pointed to the clouds that had formed over the mountains to the west. Another squall was headed their way.

He would have loved to have waited it out in a shelter, but there wasn't time. He hadn't noticed how dark this one was until now. All his thoughts had been on Lucian, on finding him, on getting the jewelry and ending this. This squall looked as if it might contain more than rain.

Geneva turned to look back at him. "You think we can reach your camp before it hits?"

He doubted it, but they had to try. Taking shelter was the smart thing to do under normal circumstances. But there was nothing normal about any of this. "We make a run for it. Wear your slicker. Don't worry about Lucky. I have her."

She nodded. "This won't be over—will it?—until the jewelry is returned. Lucian won't stop and neither will the others."

"No, it won't be over."

Tears filled her eyes. He was about to remind her that there was no crying when she said, "Thank you."

He knew she wasn't thanking him for taking care of her dog. He suspected that she'd realized that if he hadn't shown up when he did earlier, Lucian would have fired at her, and, even wounded, he would have killed her.

"I'm so sorry I involved you in all this," she said.

"If you and I hadn't already been headed up into the mountains, those three men after Lucian would have tried to get his location out of me. I might have been foolish enough not to tell them. Old loyalties die hard. So you saved my life."

She smiled at that. "Lucian said I always see a half-filled glass and think it's almost full. Seems you do too."

He returned her smile, but she was wrong. Right now, he couldn't be optimistic about any of this. He knew how much danger they were in and not just from the approaching storm.

THE DRIVING RAIN pelted her as hard as the hail that followed. Geneva ducked her head, glad for the Western hat and the slicker she wore. She kept her head down, her horse following the others through the storm.

She still felt shaken by her encounter with Lucian. Her emotions felt all over the place. She didn't want to believe that he would have hurt her puppy—let alone have killed her, but she knew soul-deep it was true. Look what the man had already done to her. Why would she think he couldn't kill to get away with it?

Ahead of her, she could barely make out the horse in front of her let alone Calhoun in the hailstorm. She could feel an urgency in the outfitter and knew that once they reached the camp, he would go after Lucian. The thought scared her. Not for Lucian but for Calhoun. Lucian had already tried to kill him, so Calhoun knew what he would be facing. But if he did go after Lucian, Geneva knew he would be doing it for her.

She also knew that the men after Lucian and the jewelry wouldn't rest until they found him and would use anyone who knew him—including her—to get that jewelry. She had every reason to be afraid, but she'd already faced down Lucian today. She'd wanted to kill him if he hurt her puppy. What kind of man would even threaten to do such a thing? He could have killed her and would have if Calhoun hadn't shown up when he did. The thought made her shudder. She'd used up all her adrenaline. Now she just felt cold and wet, tired and saddle sore.

Geneva realized with a start that the horse in front of her had stopped.

A few moments later, a wrangler came out of the storm to help her off her horse. He steered her toward a small wall tent beside the creek. "Calhoun said he'll bring your things in shortly."

She stepped inside, instantly rewarded with a rush of warm air from the woodstove in the corner. While small, she could stand up in the tent. Hail peppered the canvas top, sounding so loud she thought it would break through the fabric, then it fell silent. She could hear the men's voices coming from the larger tent she'd seen. She pulled off her wet slicker and left it and her boots and canvas pants by the door.

Shivering, she was about to strip down to nothing but her skin when the canvas door opened and Calhoun stepped in, his arms full. As he set down her puppy, Lucky came running to her. Calhoun had stopped just inside the tent. He took her in for a few moments before he quickly looked away and put down two bedrolls and a bag with her spare clothing.

"The storm has passed," he said. "There's a kettle of warm water on that stove and soap in this bag. Put on some dry clothing when you're finished and come on over to the larger of the tents. You must be starved."

Her stomach rumbled in answer, and he chuckled. When his gaze returned to her, it was warmer than the woodstove in the corner of the tent. She tried to find words of gratitude. Warm water, soap, dry clothes and food. Civilization.

But all she could think about was this man. She would be going back to Cooke City in the morning with one of the wranglers. She would probably never see Calhoun St. Pierre again. She felt an ache in her chest that made it hard to breathe. The man had saved her life. More than that, he'd gotten under her skin.

"Calhoun?" She turned, uncertain as to what she was about to say. Not that it mattered. She saw that he'd already ducked back out the door, her puppy going with him.

THE SUN HAD sunk behind the mountain, the camp full of long shadows that pooled in the pines as Geneva walked back to the small tent after dinner. The tent sat at the edge of the meadow some distance from the other tents like an afterthought. His wranglers hadn't expected him to join them and need the tent. She realized that he normally would have slept outside under the stars or in the wranglers' tent.

He'd had them set up a tent for her. And him? Calhoun had gone with his men to check on one of the horses that had come up lame. Lucky had gone with him, Calhoun promising to bring her to the tent when he came back.

A soft quiet had fallen over the camp. Several of the clients sat around the campfire talking about their day fishing one of the almost thousand high mountain lakes.

It was so peaceful that she could almost forget why she'd come up here, let alone only hours ago coming face-to-face with Lucian and how that had ended. Who was that woman who'd fired those shots? Not the Geneva Carrington Beck she'd known.

This had changed her, she thought as she stepped into

her dark tent. The only light was the glow of the stove in the corner. She could never go back to being the person she was. Unfortunately, she couldn't imagine where that left her. Or what she would do.

Earlier, she'd joined all the men in the large tent around a long portable table. She'd taken the chair she was offered across from Calhoun. He'd given her a reassuring smile when he'd seen her. But he'd also passed a message. No one but his wranglers were aware of what else was happening back up in these mountains. He wanted to keep it that way.

The clients had another two days of fishing, and then they would be headed back to town. They were a merry bunch, joking around about who caught the largest fish, who'd fallen into the freezing water of the lake, who'd panicked when they thought they'd seen a bear that had turned out to be an elk.

It had all felt so normal that she should have been able to relax while she ate. Instead, she'd been too aware of Calhoun sitting across the table from her. In a matter of days, so much had happened, of course it had formed a bond between them. She told herself not to make more of it than it was. This was Calhoun St. Pierre. He didn't take women up into the mountains. But he'd taken her.

She'd thought about the first time she'd laid eyes on him, hat covering most of his face as he'd snoozed on his porch in front of his cabin on Cooke City's main drag. She couldn't have seen where she would end up that afternoon. It hadn't been something she could have imagined.

As she stepped into the tent, she was surprised and pleased to see two cots had been set up close together given what little space there was in the small tent. She crawled up on one and lay staring up at the canvas ceiling. Pine boughs threw dark shadows over the tent, moving to the breeze. She'd dozed off when she was awakened by Lucky. The puppy jumped up on her cot, tongue lolling, tail wagging as if happy to see her. Her gaze had gone to the tent's doorway and the man standing there. Calhoun took off his hat and coat and moved toward the two of them.

"Oh, she smells like horse manure," she cried and put the dog down on the floor after hugging her for a moment.

"We call that road apples," he said grinning.

She looked up at him, happy to see that it seemed he planned to sleep here tonight. "How's the horse?" she asked as she watched him take off his jacket, then go to the woodstove to wash up with the extra water she'd left in the kettle on top.

"Nothing serious." They both fell silent as he climbed onto the adjacent cot. Lucky had curled into a ball over by the stove, seemingly content after her latest adventure.

Geneva realized how late it must be. She couldn't hear the men's voices around the campfire. The night had fallen silent. The only light was from the woodstove. She glanced over and felt a strong pull at heart level and an ache much lower.

Calhoun lay on his back. The air in the tent seemed to spark with electricity she couldn't see but could feel. Regret was a weight on her chest, because she could feel the distance growing between them even before he said, "I probably won't be here in the morning when you wake up."

Rolling up on her elbow, she looked over at him. The tent was so small, their cots were almost touching. He still wasn't looking at her. "One of the wranglers is going to take you back to Cooke. He'll take you to the barn where I left your pickup and then you can—"

"You're planning on going after Lucian, aren't you?" He didn't answer. He didn't have to. "What will you do when we find him?" she asked. He shook his head. "I don't want you to kill him." She feared what it would do to Calhoun.

He finally turned his head to look over at her. "That will depend on Lucian."

"I don't understand you," she said. "You'll carry my dog all the way up into the mountains on your horse, but when it comes to people…"

"I like animals."

"What about people?" She knew what she was really asking, *What about me?* but she couldn't bring herself to say it out loud. He'd made it clear that theirs had been a business arrangement and now it was over.

Her disappointment must have shown in her face because he added, "There's some people I like more than others." His gaze locked with hers.

"But you could kill a person."

"I could also kill an animal if it was threatening to kill me or someone I cared about."

The look in his eyes made her fall silent for a moment. "You are so passionate about so much," she said, finding it hard to breathe when he looked at her like that. "So gentle and caring and capable and yet…so stubborn, so fiercely independent, so…dangerous. I've never known anyone like you."

She was inches from him. Her desire to touch him felt overwhelming. She leaned toward him. The need to touch him so strong that—she hadn't realized that she'd reached for him until she felt his large, callused fingers close over hers gently but firmly.

He shook his head. "Bad idea."

She swallowed, her gaze still locked with his. "Are you sure about that?"

Calhoun let out a chuckle as he pushed up on his elbow so they were face-to-face. So close that their lips were almost touching. "You're scared and not thinking clearly." She shook her head in denial. "You're tempted to walk on the wild side, but you'd regret it." Again she shook her head. His eyes darkened. "You're Lucian's wife."

"All the more reason."

He laughed, shook his head and fell onto his back again. "You think you know me, but you don't." He glanced over at her. "But none of those reasons is why I'm not making love to you right now. When it happens, it won't be one night in a tent. It will be for the right reasons, and you won't be Mrs. Lucian Beck. Now get some sleep or at least let me." He rolled over, giving her his broad back.

She laid back and stared up at the canvas tent overhead trying hard not to cry. "Didn't you mean to say, *if* it happens?" He grunted, but it sounded like a chuckle. She closed her eyes. She could hear the soft crackle of the woodstove. She could smell the soap they'd both used with the kettle of hot water in their tent. Her hair was still a little damp, but she wasn't cold, her desire for this man running hot through her veins. She'd never felt more alive lying here next to him.

GENEVA DIDN'T KNOW how long she'd been asleep or what had awakened her at first. Then she heard Lucky whine over by the tent door. "What is it, girl?" she whispered as she slowly climbed off the end of the cot, careful not to wake Calhoun. He was snoring softly as she moved to the puppy and opened the door to let her out.

Worried that something might get the puppy, Geneva stepped out into the night while Lucky did her business. The night was darker than usual, clouds hiding most of the stars. She hugged herself against the cold even though she was wearing her clothes. She thought of that negligee she'd been planning to wear the night of her anniversary party. How her life had changed. Here she was sleeping in her clothes that smelled of woodsmoke, leather and horses.

The thought made her smile as Lucky came charging to her, busting through the tent door as if anxious to get back to her spot by the fire.

As Geneva started to step back toward the tent, she heard a sound. Before she could turn, she was grabbed from behind. A large hand clamped down over her mouth as she was lifted off her feet. She didn't recognize the harsh whisper at her ear, but she understood the words perfectly.

"Make a sound and I will slit your throat."

Chapter Seventeen

Calhoun woke with a start, coming face-to-face with the puppy. Lucky licked him on the nose, then whined. He sat up, aware of two things instantly. The tent door was partially open, a cold breeze coming in, and the wood-stove fire had gone out.

He quickly rolled over to find the cot next to him empty. In an instant, he was on his feet, pulling on his boots. He had no idea what time it was, only that it was still dark outside, but daylight wasn't far off. He told himself that Geneva had just stepped out to pee. She wouldn't go far.

But why hadn't Lucky gone with her?

Trying not to panic, he moved quickly to the door and looked out into the gray darkness. He didn't want to set off an alarm in camp—not until he was sure. "Geneva?" he called quietly. Then a little louder. He could hear the breeze in the pines but nothing else.

Ducking into the tent, he grabbed a flashlight and hurried back outside. He had no idea how long she'd been gone. Worse, why the puppy hadn't gone with her. It didn't take him long to realize that Geneva hadn't just stepped out to pee. He found drag marks in the still damp earth that led from the tent into the pines.

It took a little longer to find the tracks into camp and

where the two horses had been tied up not far from their tent. Not the horse Lucian had been riding or the spare horse he'd brought up into the mountains. Calhoun knew those tracks.

No, these had to be the men after Lucian. *But why take Geneva?* he asked himself even as he feared he already knew as he hurried back to the tent to scoop up Lucky. He'd slept in the tent with her because he'd been worried about her, and yet someone had still taken her. He'd thought he could keep her safe. He'd been a fool, telling himself he was taking the high road last night not making love to her. If they had pushed the cots together, he would have been holding her in his arms. He would have awakened when she got up.

Silently berating himself, he carried the dog over to the wranglers' tent, opened the door and awakened his men. "Take care of the dog. Someone's taken Geneva. I'm going after them."

He closed the tent door. It didn't take him long to get his horse saddled, but it had seemed interminable. Once in the saddle, he checked to make sure his rifle and sidearm were loaded, then he began to track the person who'd taken her, knowing that before this was over, he would have to kill—or be killed.

GENEVA TRIED TO BREATHE. The bandana the man gagged her with tasted vile. Worse, he'd tied her hands to the saddle and taken her reins as he'd led her back through the pines away from the camp. The one time she'd tried to scream for help, he'd punched her, almost knocking her out.

"Do that again and I'll leave you here to bleed out,"

he'd whispered next to her ear as he tightened the rope on her wrists until she let out a muffled cry.

His chuckle told her everything she needed to know about the man who had abducted her. Bound the way she was, she could see no way to escape. Any attempt would be met quickly with a painful response from him. Heart in her throat, she told herself to be careful while hoping for a chance to get away.

Terrified as to what he planned to do to her, she tried to rein in her frantic thoughts. She thought of Calhoun and Lucky and fought tears. She needed to keep her wits about her. This had to be one of the men after Lucian. She couldn't imagine why he would have abducted her otherwise. But where was he taking her? And for what purpose? By now, Lucian would have gotten away with the jewelry. Surely this man didn't think she had it—or anything to do with Lucian, did he? Or even more ridiculous that he could use her to make Lucian give up the jewelry?

Was Lucian even still alive? She remembered all the blood at the spot where he'd been standing. Calhoun said she hadn't killed him. But then again, Calhoun might not have wanted her to know the truth—that her shot had been fatal and that Lucian had died alone out in the woods.

Calhoun. Just the thought of him made her heart ache. He had stirred something in her, making her want not just to move on from her no-count husband and her fake marriage, but also to survive to, as the outfitter had said, take a walk on the wild side with him. She feared that would never happen, but it gave her hope that it still might. If she could get away.

Ahead, she heard a horse whinny. As they rode into a

camp, she saw two men huddled on the ground next to a campfire that had burned down to only wisps of smoke.

"I thought you were going after Lucian," one of the men said.

That she'd been right and that this man was one of the three who were also looking for Lucian gave her no satisfaction.

She thought about Calhoun. What would he do when he woke and found her gone? He'd come looking for her. If anyone could find her, it was him. She thought of her puppy but knew he would also take care of Lucky. If he could, he'd take care of her.

But first, he'd have to find her before it was too late.

BLADE WAS GLAD that he'd gagged and tied the woman to the horse. In retrospect, he wished he'd done the same thing to Ricki and Juice, given how quiet this ride had been compared to the ones with his so-called partners. The sun was coming up, turning the sky to the east a bright orange by the time he reached the makeshift camp where he'd left his cohorts. The campfire had burned down, both men had been asleep when he rode up and had let the fire go out.

He swung off his horse next to Ricki on the ground and gave him a swift kick. His yelp woke up Juice. "Get up. We're leaving."

"Can't we wait until the sun is all the way up," Juice whined. "We won't be able to see in the trees. I'm hungry. I can't keep doing this without food."

Blade moved swiftly to the man, his horse's reins in one hand, the knife in his other. Moments before, they'd been one horse short for the trip out of here. He pointed that out to Juice as he plunged the knife into the man's neck.

He heard a sound come from the gagged woman still tied to the horse as Juice dropped to the ground, blood spurting from his neck.

"What the hell, Blade?" Ricki demanded.

He swung around to face him. "You want some of this too?" Ricki took a step back, holding up his hands. "Good. Now let's get moving. You bring up the rear."

Ricki looked skeptical. "What are you planning to do with *her*?"

"She's Lucian's wife."

"What kind of answer is that? I thought we came here for the jewelry."

Blade was sick of answering to these two. He thought about leaving Ricki here as well but realized he still might need him.

"If this is about getting even with Lucian—"

"I don't have to explain myself to you. I'll do whatever I want with her. Now move."

Blade hadn't planned to take her. He'd seen where their tracks had headed back to the camp he and his men had stopped at yesterday. It was Lucian's tracks that had headed down the mountain, then stopped. The storm had hit, and Blade had lost him. They'd waited out the storm and built a fire to warm up.

He'd gotten to thinking that Lucian might have circled back. He was pretty sure that Lucian was wounded. He'd found blood droplets on his trail. Maybe Lucian had gone to that outfitter's camp for help.

But he could find no sign that his back-stabbing former partner had been there. Blade had been contemplating what to do when he'd seen the woman come out of a tent at the edge of the encampment. He'd realized that this had to be Lucian's wife, the woman he'd heard about back in Cooke City. He decided to take her, use her if needed to deal with Lucian—or anyone else who tried to stop them.

"Lucian can't be that far ahead of us," Blade said, hating that he had to spell everything out to Ricki. "That storm had to hold him up just like it did us."

He started to saddle up again, when he caught movement out of the corner of his eye.

The first shot hit with a dull thud in the middle of Ricki's chest. He made an *ooufft* sound and dropped to his knees. The second shot caught Blake in the leg as he was trying to tell from what direction the gunfire was coming from.

He grabbed his horse and, foot in the stirrup, was pulling himself up when the third shot hit him in his shoulder. He fell back, his boot tangled in the stirrup as his horse reared. The rope was still wound around his saddle horn from the woman's horse. That horse also began to rear as Blade frantically tried to free his boot from the stirrup.

CALHOUN FOLLOWED THE trail the horses had left, using his flashlight. Still the going was slow. Not just that, his light could be seen from a distance. Whoever he was following would know exactly where he was. It would be easy to walk into a trap or, worse, be ambushed before he could get to Geneva.

He knew he had to be getting close. Whoever had taken her couldn't have gotten that much of a lead. He cursed himself for bringing her up here. What had he been thinking? He reminded himself that he hadn't known about the jewelry theft. Nor had he realized how much trouble Lucian was in. He'd gone past having a friend who wanted to punch him for what he'd done or even three bikers who wanted to kick the daylights out of him as well.

Lucian had graduated to the big leagues. Hardened men out of prison who he'd double-crossed no doubt wanted to kill him.

The worst part was that he'd gotten Geneva involved. Tricking her into marriage, deceiving her, taking everything before he left her wasn't bad enough; he had to leave behind his pickup, where she would find his past and track him to Cooke City, Montana. Even if he hadn't meant to, this was all on him.

Last night, he'd planned to go after Lucian at first light. He hadn't wanted to leave Geneva, his mistake. As it was, he'd lost her on his watch. He'd never forgive himself for that. Being caught in the landslide and the rest had left him exhausted and in pain. He'd fallen into a bottomless sleep filled with nightmares and awakened to her gone.

He'd failed her when the last thing she needed was another man she couldn't depend on. Last night it would have been so easy to make love to her. He was thankful now that he hadn't. He was the last thing the woman needed.

At the sound of gunshots, his heart dropped. He spurred his horse, racing toward where he thought the shots had come from, worried why whoever had taken Geneva would give away his location with gunfire.

Chapter Eighteen

Blade was bleeding badly, in horrible pain from the gun-shot to his shoulder, not to mention the one to his free leg. His other leg was twisted to the point of breaking, and if this horse should take off running… He was fighting desperately to get his boot free until he felt a shadow fall over him and reached for the gun at his hip. He got it out, but as he looked up, he saw Lucian an instant before his former cohort stepped on his wrist, leaned down, took the weapon from him and tossed it a few feet away.

"You look like hell," Blade said. Lucian did. The side of his face was covered in dried blood and so was the front of his shirt.

"You should talk," Lucian said. "Give me your knife."

Blade hesitated. He'd already lost his gun. He felt naked without his knife. If Lucian was going to kill him, then he'd just as soon get it over with.

But then again, lying here on the ground, his leg twisted painfully in that damned stirrup, what choice did he have? Lucian would shoot him before he could get his knife out and stab the lying, cheating double-crosser.

He worked the blade out of his scabbard against his wounded leg. The pain of the gunshot wound was excruciating. He promised himself that if he got the chance, he would make Lucian pay for this and everything else with hours of torture.

"Where's the jewelry?" Blade asked as he slowly pulled the knife free.

Lucian only smiled as he stepped on Blade's wrist again, leaned down and carefully pried the knife from his fingers—just as he had the gun. "What are you doing with my wife?"

Blade had forgotten about her. She tried to say something through the gag that he couldn't make out, but it made Lucian smile.

Walking over to her, Lucian cut her free of the horse, but left her hands bound. He dragged her to the ground, grimacing in obvious pain. It was clear that Lucian was hurt worse than he was pretending. Frantically she worked at the gag on her mouth. Clearly, she had something she desperately wanted to say but couldn't get it loose with her hands bound.

"I'd leave that gag where it is," Blade advised as he felt his foot slip a little in his boot. "From the look in her eyes, she doesn't like you any more than me." If he could pull his foot out and free his leg… He kept his eye on Lucian. Just a little more and he'd be free. Then it wouldn't take much to get the gun Lucian had so carelessly tossed aside.

CALHOUN HAD ONLY one thing going for him, he told himself. The element of surprise. He knew the risk. It could just as easily get him killed. Even as he raced toward where he thought the gunshots had come from, he knew he might be too late. Geneva could already be dead. The thought sent a molten fire of anger through his veins. He would kill the bastards.

As he burst through the pines, he had his gun drawn. It took him only a few moments to assess the situation. There were unmoving bodies on the ground. Several horses. One man on the ground.

But his focus was on Lucian. He had Geneva. She was gagged and bound. But she was alive. For the moment.

Lucian raised his gun and fired a shot as Calhoun leaped off his horse a few yards away, taking cover. The bullet missed him but not by much. He saw Geneva try to get away, but Lucian pulled her into a headlock, turning so her body shielded his own.

"Calhoun," he called as he put the gun to her head. "You don't want to get this woman killed, so come on out. Let's talk about this."

"Let her go, Lucian. You've hurt her enough. This is between you and me."

Lucian shook his head. "I feel bad about what I did to you."

"I doubt that."

"Truth is, I always wanted what you had. But you should know that. Now it appears you want what I have. Funny how things work out, isn't it?"

Calhoun wanted to keep Lucian talking until he could get a clear shot. But the man who'd been on the ground was moving, working his way toward one of the bodies nearby. Going after a gun?

He swore under his breath. "That's bull, Lucian. You've stayed in my cabin. You can't have been jealous of what I have."

"You have the life you want. I've never had that. I've

finally got a chance now. But only if I get to walk away from here. Only if you help me."

"You don't look good," Calhoun said as he saw the man belly-crawling closer to something on the ground.

"You're the second person who's pointed that out," Lucian said with a chuckle. "I'll tell you what. You come out, hands up, gun on the ground, and I'll let her go. You can both ride out of here. Just let me do the same."

It was a tempting offer, but he didn't believe him for a minute. Nor could he let the other man get to a weapon. The fool would either try to kill him or Lucian. With Lucian holding Geneva the way he was, the man couldn't get a clean shot at Lucian any more than Calhoun could. The difference was the man didn't care if he killed them both. In fact, Calhoun figured his plan was to kill all of them.

Unfortunately, he couldn't get a clear shot through the horses and bodies to stop the man. Any moment, the man would reach the weapon on the ground, roll over and begin firing.

"Your friend is going for a gun," Calhoun said.

Lucian only smiled, his weapon still pointed at him.

Calhoun realized there was only one way he could save Geneva. "I'm coming out," he announced and tossed his gun out. "Let her go." He rose slowly, hands in the air, his gaze on Geneva's terrified expression as Lucian shoved her away, his gun coming up to fire.

Out of the corner of his eye, Calhoun saw the other man reach the weapon, roll to his back, the gun in his hand as he turned the barrel toward Lucian and fired seemingly at the same time as Lucian pulled the trigger.

Calhoun dove for his gun, his gaze drawn away from

Lucian and the weapon that had been pointed at his chest. He hit the ground and came up armed again. His gaze going first to where Geneva had been standing. She wasn't there. She was on the ground.

He looked at Lucian, surprised to see him sway on his feet. His gun was still held in front of him, but not pointed at Calhoun. It took a moment to realize what had happened.

Lucian hadn't fired at him. He'd shot the other man, but that man had gotten a shot off, and Lucian had taken it in the stomach.

Calhoun rushed to him, afraid Lucian would turn the gun on him or, worse, Geneva. He wrenched the weapon from his former friend without a struggle as Lucian slumped to the ground, his back to a stump.

Calhoun scrambled over to Geneva, still afraid that she'd caught one of the bullets. Her eyes filled with tears when she saw him. "Are you hit?" She shook her head. Still, he checked her over quickly, assuring himself that she hadn't been caught in the crossfire.

He helped her take off the gag, then pulled out his knife and cut her hands free. She threw her arms around him, and he held her for a long moment before she released him, and he rose to make sure the man Lucian had shot was dead.

All three of the men in the camp were dead. He moved to Lucian, seeing at once that his wound was fatal. Had they not been miles back into the mountains and even further from a hospital, Calhoun still doubted he would have made it. There would be no saving him. Geneva must have realized it as well. She sat, arms around her knees, crying softly.

Calhoun crouched down next to him. The side of the mountain had fallen into a deep silence as the sun rose above the peaks. Rays wove through the pines, chasing away the dark shadows.

"You are one stubborn bastard," Lucian said.

"Funny, someone mentioned that recently."

Their gazes locked. "She's too good for you."

Calhoun nodded. He could see Lucian's lifeblood seeping out into the dirt on this mountain range he had once loved. "Where's the jewelry?"

"Does it matter now?"

Probably not, he realized. There were more important questions he wanted to ask. "Did you love her?" What he really wanted to know was if Lucian would have killed both him and Geneva.

"What do you think? I know you'd hoped to see me behind bars. Not going to happen. I'm going to die here. Poetic, huh?"

"You're wrong. I never wanted any of this for you."

Lucian smiled through his pain. "But you want my wife." His laugh was a blood-filled gurgle as he grabbed Calhoun's arm. "Take care of her."

He stared at a man he had loved as a friend and watched the life fade from his eyes, and his grip loosened. Lucian's arm dropped to the ground next to him.

Calhoun sat back for a moment before he closed Lucian's eyes and moved to Geneva.

"Is he...?"

He nodded and pulled her to him. "He saved our lives, you know?" Overhead, he heard a helicopter. His men had called in backup. He tried to breathe, caught between simply being thankful to be alive and wishing it hadn't ended this way. There was so much he had wanted to ask Lucian, starting with why he hadn't killed him when he'd had a second chance. Why he'd married Geneva, then betrayed her. Why he'd asked him to take care of her, the woman who had wanted to believe there was good in Lucian probably to the end. He'd jeopardized their lives, but at the last second, he'd saved them both.

He'd had the jewelry, he was getting away, so why had he come back? All Calhoun knew was that Lucian had died, and he and Geneva were alive because of it.

The chopper touched down in a meadow some yards away. He liked to think that Lucian had realized that no one would be safe as long as his former partners in the heist were alive and that he'd come back to save the woman he'd loved after taking everything from her but her life.

That was the problem with Lucian. It was hard to nail down what he was, other than a walking contradiction. He'd brought violence and death to these mountains that he loved. He'd also ended his lifelong battle within himself here. Calhoun liked to believe that Lucian had finally found peace.

He helped Geneva up from the ground as law enforcement officers rushed toward them.

Chapter Nineteen

Geneva heard the sound of a pickup engine in front of the cabin. She'd gotten up with Lucky, taken her out, fed her, and then they'd both gone back to bed. Yesterday when she'd finally been released from the authorities and allowed to go to the cabin Calhoun had rented for her, all she'd wanted was a shower and to sleep on a bed. She'd thought she could sleep for days.

But her sleep was fraught with real-life nightmares. Awake, she went from numb to dazed to shocked to heartbroken. She couldn't bear to think about Lucian. She had watched him die feeling nothing and yet feeling everything. She'd chased him to Montana, her motives not even clear to her. If her goal had been to find out who she'd married, she'd done that, and yet... Calhoun had said that Lucian saved their lives after putting their lives in danger.

Lucian Beck was a criminal who appeared to be soulless, but he'd saved her and Calhoun up in the mountains. How did she deal with all that knowledge about the man she had loved and married and had never really known?

She had forced herself to rise from bed, shower and dress, knowing that she had to face it all and move on. She would have days on the road with Lucky to deal with her grief, her loss and her regret. She was broke and a widow. Her husband, a known criminal, was dead. She wasn't sure she would ever trust her best friend again. And then there was Calhoun.

At the sound of the truck's engine, she picked up Lucky and walked to the door. Just seeing Calhoun standing next to Lucian's pickup lifted her heart before dropping it again. She would always think of the pickup as Lucian's. Would she always think of Calhoun as Lucian's once good friend and remember the last day in the mountains with pain and heartbreak? It was a reminder she didn't need or want, bringing up the image of Lucian dying before her eyes and Calhoun holding her as if he never wanted to let her go.

Calhoun must have seen her expression. "You can sell the pickup here in Montana and fly back to San Diego with Lucky. I can take care of selling it for you."

Geneva smiled. Sometimes the man seemed to know her better than she knew herself. He had to know that it wasn't just the pickup that was the problem. This man had saved her life. She'd put his in danger. "How are you?"

"I'll live," he said and she could see what the past few days had done to him as well. But his look said he was more worried about her. Lucky squirmed in her arms. The moment she put her down, the dog bound off to him.

Calhoun smiled as Lucky leaped into his arms. Geneva watched him pet the dog, knowing that Lucky would miss him as much as she would. In a matter of days, the man had made his mark on both their lives. Maybe she and Lucky had done the same to him.

Or maybe he would be relieved to see them both gone, taking the bad memories with them. He could now get back to his life. She wondered, though, if he would be haunted by what had happened up in those mountains. She knew she always would. She'd seen the life that her husband had lived, running from trouble, and a part of him knowing it would catch up to him one day. She couldn't imagine what demons he'd lived with without her even knowing.

Calhoun put Lucky into the pickup's front seat and met her gaze. "You must be anxious to go home."

"Yes," she lied, her eyes burning with unshed tears. The first thing she had to do was put the house up for sale. "I still don't feel right about taking the reward money." Unfortunately, everything he'd stolen from her was gone to pay off other people he's cheated who wanted him dead.

"It's what Lucian wanted," he said. "With that and the money from the sale of the truck, will you be all right?"

"I'll be fine. You don't need to worry about me anymore."

His look seemed to say that wasn't possible. Calhoun glanced away for a moment before his eyes returned to hers. "Going to take a while to sort it all out, huh?"

She knew exactly what he was saying. She had so many emotions running rampant right now. She wasn't sure how she felt about anything. Except for Calhoun. That she knew heart deep. "Thank you."

He smiled at that. "For almost getting you killed?"

"For taking me up in the mountains. For saving my life. For…everything." She held his gaze. "I'm sorry I involved you in my mess. I owe you my life."

He shook his head. "I'm sorry about Lucian. At least now you know that he loved you."

"In his way." In the end, Lucian had surprised them both, but his change of heart couldn't save him. "I'll never forget the days I spent up in the mountains with you," she said, her voice breaking.

He had no idea how hard it was to walk away thinking she would never see him again. But now she had to go back and face the past while figuring out what she was going to do in the future. "Thanks for the offer about selling the truck, but I think I need to drive. Lucky and I could use a long road trip right now."

Calhoun held out the pickup keys and she took them. Her fingers brushed his, sending sparks flying. He pulled back, looking uncomfortable. "If you ever get back this way…"

Geneva smiled, feeling tears flood her eyes. She made a quick swipe at them, determined not to cry. She had come here for answers. She'd gotten most of them. She hadn't known Lucian and never would understand why he'd done the things he had. Lucian was dead. So were their dreams.

She was no longer that woman who'd awakened the morning after her anniversary party scared and alone. She would never be that woman again. But she knew it wouldn't be easy going back, facing everything—especially her feelings for Lucian, for Mitzi and most of all, for Calhoun.

Her heart felt as beat up as her body did right now. She wasn't sure she'd ever be able to sort out everything. She and Calhoun had their own histories with Lucian and a few days together in the mountains where they'd both faced their own mortality. Not the kind of bond a person built a relationship on. She figured Calhoun couldn't wait to put the entire experience behind him.

"I would imagine that you're headed back up in the mountains," she said to fill in the suddenly very heavy silence that fell between them.

"I have clients leaving and another batch coming in," he said with a nod, but he didn't sound happy about it.

"Lucky and I should get going. You're burning daylight."

He smiled at that. "I'll never forget you." The words seemed to come out as if against his will. He pulled off his hat and kneaded the brim in his hands for a moment, dropping his gaze to the dog. "If you ever need anything…"

"I know where to find you. You have my number and I have yours."

He nodded and put his hat back on. His look confirmed what she already knew. Neither of them would be calling the other.

"Let me help you with your bags," Calhoun said.

Geneva went back into the cabin and brought out her two small duffels that she'd packed for what she'd thought would be a quick trip. He took them from her and loaded them behind the pickup's bench seat before giving Lucky another hug and closing the door.

"Calhoun—" Her voice broke and she couldn't continue.

He stepped to her, taking her in his arms and holding her against him tightly for a few moments before he stepped back. "Drive careful."

She could only nod, move to the pickup and climb behind the wheel. She tried not to look at him standing there as she worked the key into the ignition and started the engine. She saw that he'd filled it up with gas. She looked up at him and mouthed, "Thank you." Their eyes locked, and she felt a chunk of her heart break off and drop to her feet.

At the sound of motorcycles pulling up, she turned to see Ace and his friends. Ace looked as if his injuries were healing. He gave her a nod, and out of the corner of her eye, she saw Calhoun walk over to talk to them.

Shifting the pickup into Reverse, Geneva backed out, then pulled onto the road at the first break in the traffic. She looked back once to see Cooke City in her rearview mirror. Then she went around a curve, and it was gone.

CALHOUN WATCHED HER drive away and swallowed the lump that had formed in his throat. His chest ached. Hell, his whole body ached. He was still limping a little from the rockslide that had almost killed him. But that pain was nothing like watching Geneva drive out of his life.

"Go after her," Ace said from where he was straddled on his bike.

Calhoun had forgotten the bikers were there. "And say what?" He shook his head, telling himself to get over it. He had work to do. Weeks of clients coming in before the first snowstorm, before the season ended and winter settled over Cooke.

"Tell her that she got under your skin, man, that you don't want her to go."

He glanced over at Ace. "Have you seen my cabin? How about my lifestyle? There's a reason I don't have a woman in my life."

"Or did you adopt this lifestyle to make sure there

wasn't a woman in it?" Ace asked. "You were never serious about Dana, and she sure as hell wasn't that serious about you. When you walked away from her, you weren't feeling what you are now, were you?"

Calhoun laughed. "When did you become a life coach?"

"It's pretty obvious that you don't want her to go. We all saw you mooning over her."

"I knew the woman for only a matter of days. No one falls in love that fast. Nor do I have time for this." He started to walk toward his cabin, where his stock truck was parked, already loaded with supplies for his next clients. Truth was, he didn't have to go back up in the mountains with these out-of-state fishermen. His wranglers and assistant guide could more than handle it.

But he knew he couldn't stay here in town. For the first time in his life, there was no place he could go to outrun the way he was feeling.

"You're making a mistake," Ace called after him.

Calhoun stopped to look back at him. "Admit it, you just want the pickup."

"I forgot about that," Ace said, his smile exposing the broken teeth. He hadn't said who'd done the damage to his face, but Calhoun could guess. He'd met Blade.

"She's going to sell it once she gets back to California."

The biker shook his head. "I just like the idea of how much Lucian would have hated me driving it. He's really gone?"

Calhoun nodded. "He saved my life and Geneva's. It cost him his own. I like to think it was as selfless as he'd ever been. But then again, he might have realized that he wasn't going to be able to get away because of his injuries and had nothing more to lose."

"Did you see the jewelry?" Ace asked.

He shook his head. "And before you ask, I didn't get the reward for its return. I saw that Geneva got it. She'd lost everything, almost including her life because of Lucian. He owed her."

Ace snickered and looked to his friends. "Right, Calhoun doesn't care anything about her."

He laughed and walked away shaking his head. The last thing he needed was to be taking romantic advice from Ace. He needed to get back into the mountains, he thought, even as he knew he'd never be able to escape thinking about Geneva. He wouldn't be able to lay out under the stars without looking over to see her lying close by, looking up with that kind of awe that had pried his heart wide open to her.

Chapter Twenty

The days on the road driving back to California had helped. Geneva knew that she'd needed them. The long hours formed a bridge from Cooke City to San Diego, a transition from a life nothing like the one she'd known to what was waiting for her at the place she'd once felt at home.

On the way, she called a Realtor she knew and told her to put the house on the market. She realized that she didn't want the furniture. All she wanted was her belongings, and she could walk away without looking back.

But in the meantime, she had little choice but to go back and face the music, as her father would have said.

It felt as if she'd been gone for months as she parked the pickup in the garage and went inside the house. The place felt different. This time, Lucian really was gone. She didn't see him standing in the kitchen or lying next to her in the huge bed. He came to her in her dreams and only in passing. It was Calhoun who haunted her days and nights. When she ached to be held, it was him she thought of, which made her feel guilty. How could she forget her husband, who she'd been with for over a year, compared to Calhoun, who she knew such a short time?

She'd been back a few days when she heard a vehicle

pull into the circular drive and stop. For an instant, she thought of the two men who'd come looking for Lucian. But when she looked, she saw it was Mitzi. She'd thought about calling her when she'd gotten back, but she hadn't been sure what she wanted to say.

Opening the door, she saw at once how nervous the normally self-confident, devil-may-care Mitzi was standing there, her back to her. At the sound of the door opening, Mitzi swung around. There was so much pain in her expression that Geneva couldn't help herself.

She stepped to her old friend and pulled her into a hug. Mitzi hated crying, especially in front of anyone, so Geneva was surprised when she began to blubber.

"Come on in before the neighbors see you," she joked since there were no close neighbors. Still she knew her friend was embarrassed. She led her into the kitchen. "You still drink coffee?" she asked as she took down Mitzi's favorite mug she always drank out of when she came to visit.

Mitzi made a sniffling sound, grabbed a paper towel and blew her nose before pulling up a stool. Geneva handed her the mug full of coffee and watched her friend cup it in her hands as if needing the warmth. "I know what you must think of me," she said, sounding as if she might start crying again.

Geneva shook her head. "You made a mistake. You went for the brass ring without thinking of the consequences. Remember? I know how convincing Lucian could be. How are things going with Hugh?"

Her friend's face fell. "Not good. He'll never trust me ever again, not that I blame him." She blew her nose again, then added, "He's been better about money. I think things are going to be all right. Eventually. What about you? Did Lucian take everything?"

She nodded. "The house is for sale. I never liked it anyway. It was too big for the two of us, but Lucian loved it." She thought about him saying that they would fill it with children. There were still those painful reminders of the dreams he'd crushed, but they came more seldom and hurt much less as the days went on. "The jewelry was found."

Mitzi's interest peaked, just as Geneva knew it would.

"I have the reward money. It's enough to hold me over until I sell the house, find somewhere small to live and get a job."

"Wait, you got the reward money? I know you said you left, but where did you go?" Mitzi leaned forward, elbows on the kitchen island as she looked at her with a kind of awe.

Geneva topped their coffee before taking a seat at the island next to Mitzi. "I went to Montana." She told her about finding the pickup and clue about a past she also hadn't known about.

"Calhoun St. Pierre," her friend said. "He was some kind of mountain man?"

She smiled to herself. "He's an outfitter. He takes people up into the mountains to fish, hunt, hike, camp. So, yes, I guess he is a mountain man." She told her about riding horses for days on end, sleeping under the stars, eating venison in the main camp with the wranglers and clients.

Mitzi shook her head. "I can't imagine you doing any of that."

"Me neither."

"And you found Lucian and the jewelry."

"I was abducted, gagged, tied to a horse and taken to another camp. Lucian showed up. It was the second time I'd seen him. The first time—" she looked up at her friend "—I shot him."

"What? With what?"

"A gun Calhoun had left with me. I thought Lucian was going to shoot me. I think he planned to. Anyway, Calhoun showed up and Lucian got away that time."

Mitzi was shaking her head. "I can't even imagine what you've been through."

She told her about the three men Lucian had pulled the jewelry heist with and apparently double-crossed since he ended up with all the jewelry. "He hid it in the mountains, I guess, always planning to go back for it. I think his past misdeeds kept catching up to him." Geneva fell silent for a moment. "I was there when Lucian died."

"I'm so sorry. I can't believe what you went through. It's amazing that you survived it."

"It was something I will never forget," she said with a sigh and took a sip of her coffee. "Just being in those mountains, seeing that night sky. The air up there is so... amazing." She shook her head and saw that Mitzi was giving her a look she recognized only too well.

"Calhoun St. Pierre?"

Geneva couldn't help but smile. "I've never met anyone like him. Irascible, impatient, obstinate and yet so gentle, so caring, so capable of just about anything. He saved my life."

"Wow. So, do you think you'll ever see him again?"

She shook her head. "There's no room in his life for a woman. He spends most of his time up in the mountains with horses and clients. I was the only woman client he's ever taken up there, and I'm sure I'll be the last."

Mitzi seemed lost in thought for a few minutes. "Lucian really did love you."

Geneva nodded. "As much as he could love, I agree. In the end, he came back to face the men he'd done the jewelry store heist with as if he'd known they would come after me—which they did. It cost him his life."

Her friend was shaking her head. "I've always envied your life, but never more than I do right now. You were so brave to take off to Montana like that, to go after Lucian into the mountains… You're a lot stronger than me."

"It took a lot of courage for you to go back to Hugh."

"Desperation more than anything, but it was hard to face him after everything I've done. It did change things between us. I love him more than I ever did before." She shrugged and finished her coffee. "I should go. I was worried about you," she said as she got to her feet, studying Geneva as she did. "I'm not worried anymore. You're going to be fine. I just hope you get to see your mountain man again."

"I THOUGHT YOU were going up in the mountains with clients," Ace said as he roared up in front of Calhoun's cabin, climbed off his bike and scaled the ladder leaning against the new structure going up behind the old cabin.

"I changed my mind," Calhoun said. "You know, I've been meaning to build something on the empty lots I own behind the cabin for years."

Ace stood looking out through what would be a bank of windows facing the mountains. "You're going to have one heck of a view."

He'd always planned to build into the hillside, go up a couple of stories so he had a great view, especially of Pilot's Peak, the most distinctive of the mountaintops that could be seen from town.

"Just decided to do this now, huh?" Ace said with a wink. Calhoun ignored him. For years, he'd told himself that he didn't need anything more than his small cabin. Now he found himself racing against time to get the structure he was erecting closed in before winter. "You know, I'm pretty good at wielding a hammer," Ace said.

Within hours, others stopped by to help. The house went up quickly with so many hands. When it was all closed in, roof on, windows and doors in, Calhoun threw a party to thank everyone.

"I have to ask," Ace said. "Did she ever sell that pickup?"

He shrugged. "I would imagine so."

"You haven't talked to her?"

"Nope. Get you another beer?"

Ace swore. "What is wrong with you? We all know why you're building this place. Shouldn't you at least see if she wants to live here?"

"What woman in her right mind would want to live here?" Calhoun said in answer. "This has nothing to do with her. I've always talked about building a place behind the cabin."

"*Talked* being the key word. You know, if I had to pick one person who was fearless, it would have been you. I met those men, remember? I have scars to prove it. But you rode into that camp outnumbered, knowing you might die to save that woman. Don't tell me you don't feel something for her. I don't think I would have done that for a woman I had just met. I know you're a Boy Scout, come on, Calhoun, she got to you big-time." He motioned to the house he'd help build. "Have the guts to go after her and find out how she might feel about all this."

Chapter Twenty-One

"Didn't you tell me that you always wanted to paint?"

Geneva stared at the woman standing on her door-step, then at her wrist and her new smartwatch. "Mitzi? It isn't even nine in the morning. What are you doing up this early?" she asked as her friend swept past her and into the kitchen.

They'd been spending more time together, Mitzi help-ing her get the place ready for the open house. Her real estate friend said everything had to be perfect, including when it went on the market as well as the open house.

Geneva had hated that it was taking so long. She'd wanted to be out of it, and yet she hadn't found another place to live that would take a dog. So she and Lucky had settled in for the duration. She just hoped she could get the house sold before she ran out of money.

"I'm not wasting any more of my life," Mitzi an-nounced. "I'm getting up in the morning, fixing break-fast for my husband and then planning my day. I found a painting class for us to take."

"Sounds like you're planning *my* day," Geneva said as she reached for Mitzi's mug and poured them both coffee.

"It's a watercolor class. Then I thought we would go to lunch."

Geneva couldn't help but smile. She loved this new Mitzi, and she had to admit that she'd enjoyed painting when she was young but hadn't done it for years. She'd always thought she'd do it again once she was settled and had time.

Geneva looked at her friend. "When does the class start? My Realtor is coming by later this afternoon."

"This morning."

She felt herself getting excited and, looking at Mitzi, was glad she'd been able to forgive her. "I'm glad you're my friend."

Mitzi teared up, then quickly finished her coffee. "Pick you up in thirty?" As she passed Geneva, she reached over to squeeze her hand before heading for the door.

CALHOUN KNEW HE could call Geneva. He had her cell number. But it felt as if it had been too long to suddenly call, and he had no idea what he was going to say. It wasn't like he hadn't thought about calling dozens of times. He'd talked himself out of it, telling himself it was better to leave things like they were.

He knew the city where she had lived, San Diego. But he also knew that she'd planned on going back to sell the pickup and the house. He had checked online for Lucian's truck but hadn't found it listed. Maybe she hadn't sold it. Or maybe she hadn't listed it online.

After she'd left Cooke City that morning, he hadn't called to check on her even though he now wished that he had. He'd thought it would be best if he put her behind him and let her put everything behind her as well.

He thought that's what she wanted since he hadn't heard from her either.

Now he could admit that he'd been a fool. A day hadn't gone by that he hadn't thought of her with a yearning like none he'd ever felt. In the mountains, he sensed her as if she'd left a part of herself up there with him.

There were so many real estate offices. He began calling them, telling them he was looking for a house owned by Geneva Carrington Beck and that he'd lost the information. Was there going to be an open house? For all he knew, she'd already sold it. Or changed her mind and stayed in it.

After dozens of calls, he was about to give up when he struck gold. As a matter of fact, there was going to be an open house this coming week. He didn't hesitate. He caught a flight out of Billings and headed for San Diego, arriving a day before the open house.

He had no idea what he planned to say to her. In his rental car, he put in the house's address and let the navigation system take him to an exclusive part of the city. "You have now reached your destination." He pulled to the curb and got out. Butterflies were doing cartwheels in his stomach. Was he really doing this? He checked the address again on his phone, stopping just a few yards from the rental car.

Staring at the monstrous house, he suddenly felt sick. What was he doing here? He thought of the three-bedroom house he'd built in Cooke City. It wasn't even finished yet. But even finished, there was no comparison.

He'd known that Geneva had had a pampered life the first time he saw her. Did he really think that a few days in the mountains with him would make her want something else? Would make her want him and his lifestyle?

Geneva had lived here in this mansion with Lucian, and the fool had left her. Calhoun thought again of the house he and his friends had built back in Cooke City. This, he told himself, is why he hadn't contacted her. He never should have listened to Ace. What had he been thinking, flying down here like a madman, to do what?

But as much as he knew he should drive away, he couldn't. Ace thought he was brave. What the biker didn't realize is that this was more terrifying than anything he'd ever done. With Dana, he'd asked her to marry him knowing it probably would never happen. One of them would back out. As it was, she took the easy way out by sleeping with Lucian.

But Geneva... She was so out of his league. Still, he'd come this far. He had to at least see how she was doing.

He'd say hello and catch up, and then he'd go home. Everyone would think she'd turned him down, which was fine with him.

Calhoun realized he was a bigger fool than even he had thought and started to turn back to the rental car. He should never have come here. He was delusional if he thought—

The front door of the house opened and he saw her step out. She stopped. Even from a distance, he could see that she was frowning. He felt his heart thundering in his chest. She didn't recognize him.

A blur of movement caught his eye as a black-and-white dog came barreling out. Lucky stopped just as his mistress had but then began barking. He hadn't noticed until that moment that Geneva was holding a leash in her hands. Had they been going for a walk?

Ace had been right about one thing. Calhoun had been afraid of little. But right now, he fought the urge to rush back to the rental car and drive away as quickly as possible. He could hear Geneva calling the dog back. "Lucky!"

Calhoun was moving toward the car when the dog stopped barking. When he looked up, he saw Lucky racing toward him, all wagging docked tail, floppy ears and lolling tongue. When the dog reached him, Lucky jumped around him in obvious excitement at seeing him again.

He dropped down to hug the dog to him. He'd never been so glad to be remembered—even by a dog. "How have you been, girl? I've missed you."

He felt a shadow fall over him and looked up to see Geneva standing there smiling down at him. He saw her momentary confusion, then surprise. "Calhoun?"

He'd forgotten that he'd shaved and gotten his hair trimmed. He'd also picked up a pair of trousers and a button-down shirt. The only thing he hadn't changed about his attire were his cowboy boots.

She too looked so different from the woman who'd driven up in front of his cabin all those weeks ago. That woman had hollowed eyes, a look that said she'd been beaten down by life and was angry and scared and hurting. This woman looked radiant. There were no dark shadows under her Montana sky blue eyes. Her long hair was pulled up into a ponytail. She looked young. She also looked happy.

He realized he might be bringing all the bad memories back with him. He shouldn't have come. He should have left her alone. He definitely shouldn't have listened to Ace, of all people.

"Calhoun, what are you doing here?" she asked. Her smile was as bright as the sunshine-filled day.

He opened his mouth, almost afraid of what might come out, then Lucky licked him in the face. "She's gotten so big," he said. "I didn't think she would remember me." He met Geneva's gaze. "I figured you wouldn't either."

HE HAD A POINT. Geneva had hardly recognized him. Now, though, she couldn't help staring—or smiling. Calhoun had cut his hair and shaved off his beard. She recalled thinking that he would be more handsome without all that hair. He was gorgeous with or without the long hair and beard. To her surprise, she missed his old look.

She couldn't believe he was here. When she'd first left Montana, she'd thought she might hear from him. She'd left him her number. He'd seemed embarrassed when he'd pocketed it. He hadn't offered his own, instead saying something like, *"You know where to find me."* But she had his number since it was listed online. Still she hadn't called.

Not that she'd expected to ever hear from him again. She'd told herself that he was just glad to have her out of his life. After all, she'd made him break his standing rule of never taking a woman up in the mountains. She'd forced him into taking her and almost gotten them both killed.

"I just assumed you never wanted to see me again," she said, her throat as dry as her mouth.

Calhoun rose slowly to his full height as she attached

the leash to Lucky and ordered her to sit. Like her, the dog was too excited. Her own heart was pounding wildly. "What are you doing here?" she asked, still taken aback.

He chuckled and looked around as if unsure. "Now that I'm here?" He shook his head as his gaze came back to hers. "I don't know what to say."

She could see how uncomfortable he was. "Well, I'm glad you're here, and Lucky has already expressed how she feels. Would you like to come inside?" Calhoun glanced toward the house. She saw his expression. "It's ridiculous," she said of the house. "I never wanted it. Lucian…well, he loved it. Or we could go somewhere if you'd prefer."

His gaze came back to her, and she saw the relief in his expression. "I could use a drink if there was some place around here, but Lucky—"

"This is California. There is a bar nearby that allows dogs." She glanced at his car. "That's if you don't mind taking her in your—"

"It's a rental. I'd be honored to have Lucky ride in it." He smiled, lighting up his whole face. She'd seen how nervous, how out of place he'd felt and was glad that he seemed to be trying to relax. He still hadn't said why he was here, but she'd learned a long time ago that Calhoun St. Pierre answered questions when he was darn good and ready.

He put Lucky in the back seat and opened the passenger door for her. She slid in and tried to catch her breath. Her heart was still pounding. Calhoun was here in San Diego. He'd come to see her. She had no idea if he was just passing through town, but she didn't think so.

She looked over at him as he climbed behind the

wheel. Had he cut his hair and shaved because of her? "I miss your long hair and beard," she said as he started the car.

He shot her a surprised look and then chuckled as if he didn't know what to think of her and her taste. They fell into a companionable silence for a few moments as she told him how to get to the bar. "I thought traffic was bad in Cooke. I'll never complain about it again."

Geneva couldn't seem to keep the smile off her face. She was so happy to see him. "I'm glad you're here. How have you been?"

"Busy," he said. "Building a house."

"A house?"

"On the property behind the cabin. I always planned to but had never gotten around to building it."

"So, things are going well?"

He met her gaze, and to her surprise shook his head. "I've missed you."

She laughed, seeing how hard that was for him, this man of few words who kept his emotions tied down tighter than the packs on his horses. "I've missed you too."

He smiled then, so much like the old Calhoun that she felt her heart soar.

"You're doing well," he said. She could feel him studying her as he drove.

She met his gaze. "I'm doing okay."

"Do you have a place to live once your house sells?"

"Mitzi, my old friend, has offered me their guest-house for as long as I need it."

"Really?" He seemed surprised by that. "The one who blackmailed Lucian?"

"That's the one. We'd been friends for too long to let the friendship go." She shrugged. "Life's funny."

"Isn't it?" They'd reached a small out-of-the-way tavern. Because it was early, the place was almost empty. Still, they sat outside under an umbrella, where they were entirely alone.

"Tell me about the house you built," she said, feeling as nervous as he looked. What was he doing here? She hated to get her hopes up and kept tamping them down, but still, him being here kept reaffirming her hope that he'd come to see her for a reason.

"The house isn't anything special. Certainly nothing like you're used to."

The bartender brought out the beers they'd ordered.

"I never wanted that house. It was too big, too much, but Lucian…" She shrugged. "I hope it sells today. That would make me very happy. I put down a large down payment. It would be nice to get that back, and I guess the market is really hot right now. My Realtor thinks the house might go into a bidding war and I'll get more than I paid for it."

"I suppose you have plans for the money, another house?" he asked.

She shook her head and cupped the beer bottle to keep her hands from shaking. "I'm not staying here." She saw his surprise.

"But you have friends here. I thought you've always lived here."

Geneva nodded. "You do realize this is the most I've ever heard you say. I thought all you ever did was grunt and answer questions in monosyllables. What are you doing here, Calhoun?" Sitting under the umbrella outside, drinks in front of them and Lucky curled up at their feet, she asked him again. "Isn't this your hunting season with clients?"

"My hired guide can handle it for a few days," he said, then picked up his drink and took a sip, not looking at her.

Okay, he wasn't ready to tell her. "It doesn't matter, I'm so glad to see you. It's a wonderful surprise."

"Did you sell the pickup?"

"Not yet. Lucky likes it too much." She shrugged, feeling foolish. "It has sentimental value, but not because of Lucian. Maybe despite Lucian. I don't expect anyone to understand, but it's become a sign of my freedom. Without it, I would never have had the courage to go to Montana, I would have never forced you to take me up into the mountains." She held his gaze. "I would have never met you." She saw the effect of her words on him.

He swallowed. "If you're not staying here, what are you planning to do after you sell the house?"

Geneva hoped she knew what he was asking. "I don't know. For the first time in my life—make that the second time in my life—I don't know what I'm going to do."

"I would think you'd buy another place, maybe not as large as the last one."

She shook her head. "I'm not really interested in doing that." A silence fell between them. "I've been taking painting lessons. My friend Mitzi signed me up. It's been fun. I've missed painting."

He raised an eyebrow. She wasn't sure which surprised him the most, her being friends with Mitzi again or painting classes.

"Eventually, you're going to tell me why you're here,"

she said as they sipped their beers. "Or do you need another beer first?"

Calhoun chuckled. "I keep thinking there is no way you could know me after just a few days in the mountains."

"Those were some few days," she said.

Lucky squirmed on the floor in the middle of a dream where she was running after something. Her legs moved, and a soft cry emitted from her throat. It must have been a good dream. Geneva reached down to pat her, and Lucky fell back into a peaceful sleep.

She felt Calhoun watching her. She'd gotten the feeling that maybe he'd come here to ask her something. Now she thought that maybe he'd changed his mind.

CALHOUN CONSIDERED THE woman across from him. She was right. What had happened between them had been so intense that they had imprinted on each other. At least that's the way Ace had explained it.

"You remember Ace?"

She raised a brow. "Your biker friend?"

"He has a master's in psychology. He tried to explain to me why I've thought about you every day since I met you and in the weeks since you left."

"You've thought about me every day?" she asked with a grin. "Funny, but I've thought about you too."

"Really?" He studied her, telling himself that she really might know him, but he knew her too. At least he knew the woman he'd spent that time with in Cooke City. Seeing her house here in San Diego and her, he'd thought she was a stranger. But she wasn't. Still, she was out of his league even if Ace had been right about there being a connection between them, one that felt strong enough that he was sitting here about to ask her—

"How long are you staying?" she asked.

"I fly back this evening. I know it's a quick trip, but…"

"You almost didn't stay to see me earlier. I was afraid you were leaving without saying a word."

He nodded, embarrassed at how close he'd come to chickening out. "I wasn't even sure you'd want to see me."

They ordered another beer as the sun went down. Calhoun would have to head to the airport soon. He'd booked a return flight for later, telling himself that once Geneva turned him down, the best thing he could do was get home.

"So, tell me more about the house you've been building," she said. "After all, daylight's burning."

He smiled, remembering how many times he'd told her the same thing. "It's a proper house on my property behind the cabin. The cabin will still be where I work out of. Clients like it." He shrugged. "It's…authentic."

"Like you."

He grinned at that and rubbed his jaw, thinking how unauthentic he felt being here dressed the way he was in dress pants and shirt. He hadn't been able to give up his boots though, but he'd left his hat at home.

"So, this house," she said, when he hesitated.

"Three bedrooms, running water, heat and a view I think you'd like," he said, warming to his subject. "A person could live there year-round, but wouldn't have to."

She smiled and nodded. "What would a person do in this house?"

"They could paint, or they could spend the summer

and fall in the mountains and leave in the winter. Go somewhere warm. Like…" he glanced toward the window "…like here, I suppose." He shifted his gaze back to her.

"Seems like you've given this some thought," she teased. "Ace help you out with this?"

He laughed, knowing how foolish it sounded. It felt good to laugh though. He could almost breathe, even with his heart still pounding. "Ace did say a few things that made sense. He and a lot of other people in town helped with the house. Full disclosure, it isn't finished. I thought I should get some advice from someone knowledgeable about such things as to how to finish and furnish it."

She leaned closer. "Sounds interesting. Tell me more."

Calhoun felt his mouth go dry. He shook his head and looked away for a moment before he met her gaze again. "I'd say this was the scariest thing I'd ever done, except I've already lived that when I thought I'd gotten you killed. Would you want to…? Hell, I can't believe I'm here, let alone saying this." He looked away. "I've always done okay with women." His gaze came back to her. "But you. You make me feel like the first time I asked a girl I liked to my birthday party back in grade school."

She laughed. "Are you asking me to your birthday party?"

He let out a sigh, his gaze locking with hers. "The problem is that I don't have much to offer a woman like you."

She raised an eyebrow. "A woman like me?"

"You know what I mean." He swore. "I knew this was a mistake. I shouldn't have listened to Ace."

"You're taking advice about me from your biker friend? What did he tell you to do?"

"To come down here and tell you how I feel."

Geneva leaned back and raised both palms up. "How do you feel?"

"Right now? Foolish. You and I, we live such different lives. Ace doesn't know what he's talking about."

"When you aren't feeling foolish and blaming Ace, how do you feel?"

He met her gaze and held it. "You're enjoying my discomfort."

"A little," she admitted. "If it helps, I know how you feel, like this thing between you and me happened too fast, the feelings can't be real, we hardly know each other, and yet…"

He nodded and picked up his beer. "How did this happen?"

She shook her head. "We went through a lot in the days we were together. We got to know each other quickly and rather…intimately because of it."

"We'd be fools to rush into anything," he said. "I mean, even if you wanted to come back with me to Cooke to see if it could work, you might hate it, you might realize you didn't like me anymore than you liked winter there, but to ask you to just come with me…"

"If you're asking if it will take marriage to get me to go with you…" She shook her head, still looking amused by his dilemma. "Here's a thought. Maybe we should at least kiss again. Maybe there isn't any chemistry anymore and your problem is solved."

He chuckled, seeing that she was teasing him. But he

did relax a little as he leaned toward her. He'd wanted to kiss her from the moment she'd come out of her house.

MITZI WOULD HAVE called it the Kiss Test. Only Geneva wasn't worried. This was one test she knew they would pass. She remembered the kiss up on the mountain. It had kept her going from the day she drove away from him until this moment.

Calhoun drew her to him, gazes locked, and then he kissed her, stealing her breath, sending her heart off at a gallop. The chemistry had only grown stronger. It was like lightning high in the mountains. It rattled through her, igniting desire and passion and sending a fiery heat to her center.

When they finally pulled apart, they were both breathing hard. She could tell that Calhoun had felt it as well.

"Looks like we're getting married," she said with a laugh. Before she could tell him she was only kidding, he pulled her to him and kissed her again.

"I'm just afraid you'll be disappointed. In the house. Or in me."

"Don't you realize by now that the only way you could have disappointed me was by not staying to see me today? Trust what you learned about me in Montana, not what you think you see down here in San Diego."

Calhoun took her hand. "I haven't been able to get you off my mind. You're all I've thought about. I've never felt like this. I want to marry you, but don't say anything right now."

"Calhoun—" her voice broke.

"Just listen." He took a breath. "Since the day I met you, I've done things I swore I would never do. What is it about you?" She shook her head. "How can I be saying this? I'm crazy about you. I want to marry you. I want to take you back to the house I'm building and live there with you. But that's my heart talking. My head is telling me it will never work. But I want you so bad. Tell me if I'm completely off my rocker for thinking you and I…"

She shook her head. "That you and I are falling in love?" He kissed her again. The next time they pulled apart, they just looked at each other as if equally shocked by the passionate feelings between them. Her heart was pounding, and she was having trouble catching her breath. "Is this really happening?"

He nodded as if understanding how she was feeling. "I want to make you happy. Is it possible that you could be happy up there with me?"

She cupped his freshly shaven cheek. "I think I could be happy anywhere you were. You love it in Montana. You don't want to live anywhere else."

He nodded, looking miserable. "But I would leave in the winter if it's what you wanted."

"I fell for those mountains even though sometimes they were scary. I fell for your life. I fell for you, Calhoun St. Pierre. I know it seems impossible that it could happen so quickly. But it did. I've thought about you every day since I left. All I could think about was going back, but I didn't think you would want me."

He groaned again and pulled her to him. "Want you? It's all I want and that terrifies me. But I'm here. Tell me what we're going to do about this?"

That was an easy one, she thought. "We're doing this. But I have to tell you, that marriage proposal, if that's what that was?" Geneva shook her head. "I agree we shouldn't jump into this. However, I'm warning you right now. The next time you ask me to marry you, you'll need to work on your pitch."

He laughed and pulled her to him. "I can't wait until you get to Montana."

"I'll come as soon as I sell the house."

"You flying or driving?"

She grinned. "Driving."

"Oh, THAT IS so romantic," Mitzi said when she told her about Calhoun's visit. "But you can't be serious about going back to Montana. I looked that town up online. Have you seen it in the winter?"

Geneva chuckled. "I'm looking forward to it. As soon as I sign the papers on the house, it's history." It would be the last of Lucian—at least here in San Diego.

"I can't believe how much money you made on the house," her friend said. "You were so lucky to have sold when you did."

"That's me—'lucky.'"

Mitzi seemed to remember her words at Geneva's anniversary party only months ago. "I know I was jealous of you. I swear I'm not anymore. You'll invite me to your wedding, won't you?"

"We're a long way from that. I'm not jumping into another relationship. Calhoun and I are both going to see how it goes. We're both gun-shy."

"You have to admit, it's so romantic. He built a house for you."

Geneva laughed. "You might change your mind when you see it."

"I doubt that since I know how much you hated Lucian's house. It wasn't you. I'm betting Calhoun knows you better than Lucian ever did."

She liked to think that was true. "Lucky loves him and so do I, although I haven't told him. But there's going to be time."

"You're really driving to Montana in that pickup again?"

"Lucky and I like road trips. Anyway, I can take what few things I'm keeping of mine and pack them in the back. I got a camper shell for the truck. It really feels like mine now." She saw Mitzi's wistful look. "How are things with Hugh?"

"Good. When I told him about your plans, he was happy for you. He suggested we come up to see you. He's never been to Yellowstone National Park. What am I saying? Neither have I. He's suggested maybe we could travel more, something I've always wanted."

"Sounds like things are going well." She was happy for her friend. "Come visit soon." Geneva couldn't wait, knowing that, like the first time she went to Montana, this would be the adventure of her life because it would be with Calhoun.

Epilogue

It had been snowing the day Geneva and Lucky drove into Cooke City. Huge lacy flakes had fallen from the heavens as she'd parked in front of the No Parking sign in front of Calhoun's cabin. As she'd turned off the pickup's engine, she'd been thinking about that first day back in July when she'd seen the cowboy napping with his boots up on the porch railing.

That day, she'd been wondering about what kind of man Calhoun St. Pierre was and whether or not he would help her find Lucian. That day, the town had felt deserted, nothing like it had during the summer with all the traffic. Calhoun had warned her that it would get busy again come winter when snowmobiles would be roaring up and down the road. She'd sat in the pickup excited about winter.

Now, as she watched the snowfall, she smiled to herself. Just as she had that day so long ago, she loved watching it snow. It was warm in the house Calhoun had built for them. She loved the windows that overlooked the town with amazing views of the mountains. This spot was her favorite, just as Calhoun had known it would be.

She heard him come up behind her and leaned back as he nuzzled her neck. His hand went to her swollen belly to wait to feel his daughter move. She felt his content-ment, so like her own as he pulled her back against him as they both looked out at the falling snow. The forecast was for two to three feet.

It didn't matter. They weren't going anywhere for a while. Lucky trotted up beside them and rose on her hind legs to rest her feet on the windowsill and look out at the world. Cooke City in the winter was beautiful. Even the buzz of snowmobiles didn't bother Geneva. Every day in the winter felt like Christmas to her. She knew it was because she'd grown up in San Diego, where the weather was much the same every day. Up here, she loved the seasons.

She also loved this house Calhoun had built for them that looked over the town. Soon there would be more of them living in this home they'd made together. She'd loved getting to choose flooring and window coverings, as well as furnishings.

It was where they'd had their first party to welcome her to town. They'd been married here, with Ace as Calhoun's best man and Mitzi as her matron of honor. They'd celebrated almost every major event in this house.

They'd been together for six months when Calhoun had asked her to marry him. It had been right before Me-morial Day, right before the town would fill with tour-ists again for the summer season, and she and Calhoun would be going back into the mountains with clients. She loved the trips, enjoyed his clients and had learned to fly-fish on the lakes. She loved being on horseback now, feeling at home in the saddle.

It was on one of those early trips back into the mountains to check to see if the camp was ready for the first clients that he'd asked her.

The day had been perfect. Blue sky, a cool breeze coming down from the still snowcapped peaks, but warm in the sunshine. They had just ridden up and he'd gotten off his horse to drop to one knee in the new grass.

"Geneva Carrington?" She'd taken her maiden name back, telling herself that her marriage to Lucian Beck hadn't really counted.

She'd smiled at him down on one knee. "Yes?"

"You are the most challenging woman I have ever known. You've made me a better man just knowing you. When I look into those blue eyes of yours, I want to move heaven and earth—whatever it takes to see you smile, to hear you laugh. I love you, Geneva. I want to marry you. Is there any chance you'd marry me after getting to know me for the past six months?"

She'd laughed. "I thought you'd never ask."

He'd picked her up, kissing her soundly and then carrying her into the tent. Two cots had been pushed together, both covered with wildflower petals.

"Better than the first time I asked you to marry me?" he'd asked after they'd spent the afternoon making love.

"It was perfect," she'd told him snuggling against him. His beard had grown back out and so had his hair. He looked like the man she'd first met, the one she'd fallen in love with. Only now, he kept both trimmed.

"I was so afraid I couldn't make you happy here," he'd confessed.

"I've never been happier. I'm excited about opening the art gallery this summer. I had no idea there were so many artists around." She'd been painting, surprised to find a community of like-minded souls in other artists, including writers. Also, she'd been surprised that several of her watercolors had sold down at the local café— Calhoun's idea, since he said they were beautiful and showed real talent, just like her. She'd been pleased but embarrassed when he'd told her what they'd sold for.

As frugal as Calhoun had always lived, she'd been surprised to find out how much money he'd invested from his business over the years. With the money she'd made on her house in San Diego, they were more than comfortable. She loved that he was like her, believed in saving rather than spending.

"I just hope I can give you the only other thing that could make you happier," he'd said that day up in the mountains in the tent after his second proposal.

She'd looked over at him and grinned, suspecting he'd already known the news she'd been waiting to tell him. "Oh, my love, you already have."

His hand had gone to her stomach. Tears welled in his eyes as he'd kissed her. "Let's start with one, but if we get the hang of it…"

"Sure," she'd said laughing. "Maybe we could make a few more."

Now from the baby's room came the sound of crying. It was followed by a second crying child. "I believe your sons are now both awake," Geneva said. Cal was almost three. Will—named after William "Ace" Graham, local biker and friend—was two. Soon, the boys would have a sister.

"We keep this up, we're going to have to add onto this house," Calhoun joked as he went to see to their sons.

Geneva hugged the daughter growing inside her. She

loved the idea of filling this house with children. Cal and Will were already riding horses. She figured her daughter would be before long as well.

Never had she imagined that this would be her life. For a moment, she thought of Lucian. She seldom did anymore. But she couldn't help wondering if he was happy for her as if he'd had a hand in this—even though he'd denied leaving the storage unit key for her to find. She knew it was silly to think he had.

Maybe it was just fate, the way she'd met Calhoun St. Pierre.

Or maybe it was destiny.

But she was thankful that she'd had the courage after finding that old black pickup to make this trip north to Montana. Beside her, Lucky leaned against her leg for a hug. Geneva reached down to pet her and looked into those big brown eyes. "What would I have done without you?" she whispered to her faithful companion.

Calhoun came out of the bedroom with a boy in each arm. The three filled the house with laughter as they headed for the kitchen. Lucky went to join them, and Geneva followed them and the enticing scent of the elk roast Calhoun had put in the oven earlier while she had made a salad.

After he sat the boys down at the table, Calhoun turned on music and stopped to dance a few steps with her before he went to see about the roast.

Her heart filled to overflowing as he began to sing along with the music, the boys joining in. Lucky began to howl, making them all laugh.

Outside, snow fell silently. Inside, Geneva watched

her family with a kind of awe. This was all she'd ever wanted—and more than she had ever imagined.

Calhoun turned to see her standing there fighting tears and moved to her. They began to dance, hearts beating in time with the music and each other as their children watched in giggles.

Geneva had to laugh. However she'd ended up here, she couldn't have been more thankful. Her father would have approved.

* * * * *

HARLEQUIN
Reader Service

Enjoyed your book?

Try the perfect subscription for Romance readers and get more great books like this delivered right to your door.

See why over 10+ million readers have tried Harlequin Reader Service.

Start with a Free Welcome Collection with free books and a gift—valued over $20.

Choose any series in print or ebook. See website for details and order today:

TryReaderService.com/subscriptions